Snapshot

I switched out the light and backed out of the room. In the kitchen I picked up the cat basket, turned off the light and opened the door to the hall. From where I stood I could see the window of the living room. Suddenly I stopped.

Something was moving in the area. A man peered in. The lamplight from the road made him into a black silhouette, rimmed with yellow.

It was so quiet. No traffic passing up the road. Even Alias was quiet inside his basket.

Apart from my own breathing, the only sound was the scrape of a key in the front door.

SNAPSHOT

Andrew Taylor

Lions

An Imprint of HarperCollins*Publishers*

The extract quoted from the
Shorter Oxford Dictionary is reprinted by
kind permission of the Oxford University Press

First published in the U.K. in 1989 in Armada
This Lions edition first published in 1992

Lions is an imprint of
HarperCollins Children's Books, a division of
HarperCollins Publishers Ltd,
77–85 Fulham Palace Road,
Hammersmith, London W6 8JB

Printed and bound in Great Britain by
HarperCollins Manufacturing, Glasgow

Snap-shot . . . Also **snap shot**, **snapshot** . . .
1. A quick or hurried shot taken without deliberate aim, esp. one at a rising bird or quickly moving animal . . . 2. An instantaneous photograph, esp. one taken with a hand-camera . . .

The Shorter Oxford Dictionary, Third Edition.

CHAPTER ONE

It was late on the Saturday afternoon that I found Pseud's body and met the girl called Smith for the first time.

Neither experience was much fun. Of course, compared with what happened later, they were just an unpleasant taste of worse things to come.

It all began at Miss Tibberton's. The last time I saw her, she'd said I could come over on Saturday if I wanted. I nearly didn't go but, to be honest, there wasn't much else to do. All my mates seemed to be going away or doing something exciting over the Bank Holiday weekend. Everyone except Barry, and he's the sort of friend you can do without. Anyway, I needed to use her darkroom.

The rain was tipping down. I had my camera and stuff in a plastic bag. My denim jacket was soaked, and the water was running down my neck. But as I turned into the road where Miss Tibberton lived, I stopped for a moment. In Endymion Street, it pays to look who's coming. A boy at our school lost £20 and his personal stereo there on Christmas Eve. They left him lying in the gutter, and he still hasn't got his sense of smell back.

Today the rain was keeping most people indoors. Two black guys were standing on the opposite corner, deep in conversation. A tall man in a navy-blue raincoat was coming in my direction, walking fast and glancing back as he walked. He had very long legs and arms. With another set of legs and arms he would have qualified as a humanoid spider.

He stumbled over a broken paving stone and nearly cannoned into me.

"Look where you're going," he snarled.

I had a glimpse of grey eyes in a long, grey face topped with grey, bristly hair that stuck up like a brush. He looked respectable but he didn't sound it.

"If anyone needs glasses," I said as he swung round the corner, "it's you."

I walked quickly down the road, wondering if he'd heard me. On either side were terraced houses built of yellow brick. They were three storeys high, and most of them looked as though the only thing keeping them up was their neighbours. Miss Tibberton lived in number 85, about halfway down on the right.

Her house was divided up into three flats. She had the one in the basement. I went down the steps into the little area where the dustbins were. That's when I saw Pseud.

She was lying between a plastic dustbin without a lid and a cardboard box. She was on her side, with her head flung back and her legs stretched out. I'd often seen her lying like that in a patch of sunshine.

But it wasn't sunny today.

Pseud's black and grey fur glistened with rain. She hated water. Her eyes were open, and so was her mouth. The cracked concrete beneath her head was streaked with red, some of it diluted to a browny-pink by the rain.

For a moment I just gawped at her. Then I bent down and touched her head.

"Pseud," I said stupidly. "Come on, wake up."

Even as I spoke, I knew she wasn't going to wake up ever again. She was just a bag of wet fur with bones and flesh inside. There was a speck of blood on the tip of my finger and my mouth was dry.

She must have been run down by a car, I thought. It was just my luck that I was going to be the one to tell Miss Tibberton. She worshipped her cats. God knows why. Pseud's death was going to ruin my afternoon. Then I felt guilty, because it would be far worse for the old woman.

I took a deep breath and pressed the bell. A few seconds later bolts rattled on the other side of the door. It opened a few inches. A pale face peered at me through the crack. The door was still on the chain. The person behind it was at least six inches shorter than Miss Tibberton. I'd never met anyone else here before.

"Yes?" It was a girl. Her voice wasn't exactly welcoming.

"How about letting me in?" I said. "It's raining, in case you hadn't noticed."

"What do you want?"

It was then that I realized she was American. The sky was so dark that I couldn't see her properly. All I had was a vague impression of a cloud of dark hair and a pale, ghostly face. And a strong impression that she didn't want to talk to me.

"I've come to see Miss Tibberton," I said curtly. "By appointment. Is she in?"

The girl nodded. "But she's busy."

The edge of the door wavered, as if she was tempted to slam it in my face.

"Well, do you think you could manage to let her know I'm here?" By now I'd decided she was either deaf or mentally retarded, so I spoke slowly and very clearly. "If it's not too much trouble."

I didn't bother to keep the sarcasm out of my voice. Pseud's body was four feet away from me, I was soaked to the skin, and I didn't really want to be here in the first place. All in all, I was in no mood to put up with any nonsense from a stupid girl.

She sucked in her breath and for a moment I thought she was going to snap back at me. But all she said was, "Who shall I say?"

"Chris Dalham. And tell her I've got some bad news about Pseud."

"About *what*?"

"You heard," I said. "Pseud."

9

She shut the door in my face with the next best thing to a slam. If she didn't know who Pseud was, she didn't know much about Miss Tibberton. That gave me an edge over her, for what it was worth. And at least she could help me break the news about Pseud.

The girl was gone for ages. It suddenly occurred to me that maybe Miss Tibberton wasn't there, and that the girl was the lookout for a gang of housebreakers. Or even that something had happened to Miss Tibberton – the same sort of thing that had happened to Pseud. That was crazy.

All the same, I was relieved when the door opened – off the chain, this time – and Miss Tibberton glared down at me. The glare didn't worry me: it was her normal expression – after a while you got used to it.

"You said I could use the darkroom," I reminded her.

"I'd forgotten you were coming," she said, with a trace of irritation.

I shrugged. No one likes being forgotten.

Her face was triangular, with slanting eyes. She looked just the same as she always did – smartly dressed in a skirt and jacket, but somehow drained of colour. She never wore make-up and her grey hair was cut almost as short as the humanoid spider's. I used to think she was like a faded black-and-white photograph.

"What's this about Pseud?" she demanded. Miss Tibberton never wasted time on social chit-chat.

I swallowed. "I think she's dead." I half-turned, pointing at the sodden thing that lay between the dustbin and the cardboard box. "I'm sorry," I said awkwardly. "Really."

Her eyes followed my finger. If her face was an open book, it was written in a language I didn't understand. Then she took a step forward and knelt down, ignoring the wet. Her long fingers stroked Pseud's head, probing and caressing at the same time.

She looked up at me. I don't think she saw me – it was

as though I were a sheet of glass and she just happened to be staring through at something completely different. Her hand was red with blood; she wiped it absently on her jacket. There were streaks of rain, or maybe tears, on her cheeks. I hoped they weren't tears. This was bad enough as it was without having to watch Miss Tibberton cry.

"A bullet," she said unexpectedly. ".22, perhaps. Fired at close quarters. She'd let anyone stroke her, you know."

I gaped at her. Even round here they don't usually shoot cats. Tie them in a sack and drop them in the canal, maybe, but that's different. And how did she come to know so much about guns?

"But who did it?" I said.

Her eyes refocused. I'd become solid again. She didn't answer me for a few seconds.

"Hooligans, of course," she said at last. "Mindless vandals. They're two a penny round here. They're hardly human, really. I've seen them baiting the cats."

"But— "

"Hooligans," she said again, this time with a touch of firmness. Then: "I can't leave her there."

"When d'you think it happened?" I was trying to avoid looking at Pseud.

Miss Tibberton twitched her shoulders. "Not long ago." She sniffed and then looked assessingly at me. "We'll have to bury her. Will you help?"

I nodded, without enthusiasm. Miss Tibberton had the use of the back garden, such as it was. At the bottom of the jungle was a little open space with a line of cats' graves. All the graves had wooden markers, each with a name and a date. Weird names, like Doctor Dee and Negative and Coma. And now Pseud.

"You'd better come in," she went on. "I've got a spade out at the back. And I've got another favour to ask you."

We left Pseud where she was and went into the flat. I

was surprised and relieved at the same time: I'd expected her to be much more upset. Those cats were like children to her. I was also irritated that I'd been volunteered for grave-digging duty.

As soon as I got inside the front door I knew that something else was wrong. A narrow passage led up to a door at the end, Miss Tibberton's bedroom. There were two other doors on the left – the first gave on to the living room, with the bay window, and the second opened into the small kitchen. Beyond the kitchen, in a sort of lean-to, was the bathroom that Miss Tibberton used as a darkroom.

Usually all the doors were closed. Today they were open. Usually the passage carpet was spotless. Today it was littered with all sorts of rubbish – books, old newspapers, a dishcloth and a load of feathers that probably came out of a cushion. The walls of the passage were bare. There used to be four framed photos of lions on the left and six photos of panthers and tigers on the right. I told you Miss Tibberton was nutty about cats.

Then I temporarily forgot about the mess. The American girl was standing in the doorway of the living room. She was wearing a faded sweatshirt and jeans. Her eyes glanced at me and then up at the ceiling. I got the feeling I wasn't very popular. Well, what the hell.

"Have you had burglars or something?" I said.

Miss Tibberton swung round so sharply that I bumped into her.

"Burglars?" she said. "Whatever gave you that idea? I'm having a clear-out. Smith was helping me."

A clear-out? Who did she think she was kidding? But I couldn't very well tell her she was a liar.

"Smith?" I said. A safe question because the answer was obvious, if ridiculous. "Who's Smith?"

Miss Tibberton's face hardened. She looked angry – but angry with herself as much as with me, as if she'd let slip something she would rather have held back.

"That's Smith," she said, nodding towards the girl. "My . . . my niece."

I opened my mouth and then closed it. I could have sworn Miss Tibberton had once said that she hadn't any relations.

"You got a problem?" the girl asked. She raised her chin slightly, challenging me to make some flip comment about her name.

I wished I could. But I couldn't think of anything suitable on the spur of the moment. So I grinned and said, "I never met a girl called Smith before."

She pushed her fingers through the black hair. There was no colour in her face. She looked very tired. And very angry: with me or Miss Tibberton?

"I guess it's one of those once-in-a-lifetime experiences," Smith said. She emphasized the *once*.

Then, as I was working out just how much of a putdown it was, she turned on her heel and disappeared into the living room.

CHAPTER TWO

The rain eased off, and that was a pity because I didn't have any excuse for not getting started. Grave-digging isn't my idea of a fun way to spend a Saturday afternoon.

"Dig deep," Miss Tibberton said as she handed me the spade. "Two feet down, perhaps. I'd do it myself but I haven't got time."

Time? I wondered. Why's she in such a hurry?

The garden was small and full of weeds. A concrete path led down to a prickly hedge about a yard high. The graveyard was between the hedge and the brick wall that marked the back of the garden. It was the only part of the garden that didn't have any weeds. Instead it had a strip of shaggy grass, sodden with the rain.

There were seven wooden markers in a neat row, parallel to the hedge and the wall. The older ones were so weatherbeaten that you could hardly read the names. I used the spade to measure the precise location of number eight. Miss Tibberton liked nice straight lines – that was one of the first things I learned about her when I went to her photography evening class.

I cut a square in the grass as neatly as I could. The turf fell into three pieces when I lifted it out. The earth was so waterlogged that digging was hard work. Soon my shoes were smeared with mud. Not for the first time, I thought that you get nothing for free in this life: every time I used her darkroom, Miss Tibberton had a little job for me to do. Like changing the cat litter or painting the kitchen ceiling. My friends would think me crazy if they knew.

But I didn't have much choice. So many people wanted

14

to use the darkroom at school that I could hardly ever get in there. And they don't let me use the darkroom at the community centre any more, not since that fight I had with Steve and Barry during the Senior Citizens' Singalong. We were just horsing around, in fact, but the bloke who runs the centre called it "unacceptably anti-social behaviour", and that was that.

At last the hole was deep enough. Alias came down the garden path, walking almost on tiptoe because it was still wet. He looked at me. Then he looked at the pile of earth. Then he peered into the hole I'd dug for his sister. He was curious but not exactly upset. Maybe no one had told him the news.

We walked up the path together. Alias purred desperately and tried to trip me up. He's one of those macho tom cats who'll do anything for a scratch under the chin.

The kitchen window was slightly open. As I came nearer I heard Smith saying something; she spoke too softly for me to catch the words. But Miss Tibberton's reply came over loud and clear.

"I'm not leaving unless she's buried, and that's flat. And I haven't time to do it myself if we're going to catch that train."

Leaving? What about the mess in the flat? What about me using the darkroom?

Alias dived through the catflap. The conversation stopped. Miss Tibberton opened the door for me. I was just in time to see Smith leaving the kitchen. Little Miss Snooty. I thought the Americans were meant to be a democratic nation.

"You've done it?" Miss Tibberton demanded.

I nodded.

She picked up an old sheet that was lying on the table, crumpled into a ball. She cradled that bundle as if it were a baby. Her baby.

"Bring the marker, will you?" she said. "I'll do a proper one later."

The last bit sounded as though she was apologizing – not to me but to Pseud. The marker was just a bit of cardboard pinned to a stick. All it said was PSEUD-ONYMOUS, with today's date underneath.

"Pseud was short for Pseudonymous?" I said. "I never knew that."

"There's a lot you don't know."

She didn't say it in an unfriendly way – more like she was just stating a rather obvious fact – but I was riled.

"I don't know who killed her, either. I don't think it was kids."

Miss Tibberton shrugged and led the way down the path. She crouched beside the hole I'd dug and lowered Pseud's mortal remains into it. For a few seconds she stayed there, staring down at the bundle and rubbing a bit of mud on the back of her hand. She's an old woman, I know – must be in her fifties if she's a day – but just then she looked as though God had dumped another twenty years on to her shoulders.

She stood up stiffly. I shovelled the loose earth back into the hole. It didn't all fit in, of course. We were left with an untidy mound of black soil, partly covered with the pieces of turf. The grass looked like a green wig.

Miss Tibberton stabbed the marker into the mound, skewering the biggest bit of grass. The marker was askew but she didn't bother to correct the angle.

When we got back to the house, Alias was under the kitchen table, wolfing down what was either a late lunch or an early afternoon tea.

"Can I use the darkroom now?" I said.

I wanted to develop a roll of 120, and do a contact print. Black and white, of course – Miss Tibberton's darkroom didn't run to colour processing.

"What?" she said.

"The darkroom," I repeated. First Smith, now Miss Tibberton: neither of them seemed to understand plain

English. Besides, using the darkroom was the only reason I'd come here in the first place.

"I'm sorry, Chris, there just isn't time."

"But the deadline's on Wednesday."

She knew what I meant. One of the local papers was running a photographic competition to find unusual pictures of familiar features of the city. I'd taken sixteen shots on that film, and three or four of them might be usable. The first prize was £500-worth of photographic equipment, and I wanted to win it as badly as I've ever wanted anything.

"It's out of the question," she said.

"But— "

Smith barged into the room. "The cab's out front," she said, "and I've put your bag in the hall."

I might as well not have been there.

"Thank you, dear," Miss Tibberton said. She turned back to me. "I'll make it up, I promise. You couldn't use the darkroom, even if there were time." She nodded in the direction of the bathroom. "It's chaos in there."

"Part of the clear-out?" Whenever I try to say something with a sneer, it comes out as a bleat. Maybe I need more practice.

"Come on," Smith said impatiently. I hate bossy girls.

"One more thing," Miss Tibberton said. "Could you look after Alias while I'm gone? It'll only be for a day or two."

It was too much. A ruined afternoon. A ruined Bank Holiday weekend. And now she wanted me to act as nursemaid to that gross ginger cat.

"I suppose so," I said, before I could stop myself.

"Good. Can you take him home with you? He needs affection as well as meals."

Affection? All Alias ever wanted was five square meals a day and a personal masseur on twenty-four-hour call, seven days a week.

"No problem," I muttered. Making three or four trips

a day to Endymion Street would be slightly worse than having Alias at home.

Miss Tibberton was already packing two bowls and a saucer into a carrier bag. "I'll give you a tray and some fresh cat litter. Always leave him some fresh water, as well as milk, won't you?"

Somewhere outside, a car hooted.

"That's the cab," Smith said.

"I won't be a moment." Miss Tibberton swept three tins of catfood into the bag. "I try to vary his meals. Beef, chicken and rabbit, in that order. Alphabetical, you see. It'll be chicken next."

The tins brought Alias from under the table. He prodded the carrier bag with a paw. Maybe he hoped a live rabbit would shoot out.

"Naughty boy. Don't give him more than half a tin at any one time."

Alias mewed. Then he did a figure of eight around Miss Tibberton's legs and mewed again.

"When will you be back?" I said.

Miss Tibberton glanced at Smith, who was still standing in the doorway and scowling at an empty space two feet above my head.

"Next week, sometime. I'll give you a ring." She fumbled in her bag and produced a ten-pound note. "That should be more than enough. He prefers Whiskas, but if he's hungry he'll eat almost anything. As for milk, he likes Gold Top, if you can find it. I hope you won't need a vet, but if you do, call Mr Auder in West End Lane – he's in the book. He's known Alias since he was a kitten, so he— "

The doorbell rang. The driver was growing tired of waiting.

"I'll get the bags into the cab," Smith said.

Without warning, Miss Tibberton took a couple of steps sideways so she was standing between me and Smith, with her back to me.

18

"Don't talk to him," she said in a whisper I wasn't meant to hear. "Not if you can help it."

Smith glanced at me. She knew I'd heard, and she didn't like it one little bit. Now this was getting ridiculous. Why the hell shouldn't she talk to the taxi-driver? The door of the kitchen closed behind her.

Miss Tibberton swung back to me. "Now, where were we?"

"The vet."

"Yes, Mr Auder. That's about it, I think. All we need now is the cat basket."

Alias was brighter than I'd thought. As soon as he heard the words "cat basket", he made a dive for the cat flap. Miss Tibberton was ready for him. She scooped him up in her arms. Alias wriggled violently.

"Get it down, will you?" she said. "It's on top of the fridge."

The cat basket was big enough for two and made of wicker. It had a metal grille at one end. I undid the straps as fast as I could. I heard a squeal as Alias dug a claw into Miss Tibberton's forearm, but she managed to hang on to him. The worst part was making sure he stayed in the basket while we fastened the grille. It's amazing what a determined cat can do. Both of us were breathing hard by the time Miss Tibberton succeeded in buckling the last strap.

The door opened. Smith was standing in the doorway again. I pretended I hadn't seen her.

Alias spat at us one last time. Then he gave up the protest as a bad job and curled himself up on the floor of the basket. Five seconds later he seemed to be asleep. Cats are realists. If I believed in reincarnation, I'd like to be a cat next time round.

"Poor love," Miss Tibberton said, as she washed her scratch under the cold tap. "It's such an indignity for him."

"We're going to be late," Smith said.

19

"Coming." Miss Tibberton seized her handbag. "You'll keep him inside, won't you?" she said over her shoulder. "I'd better leave you a key in case he does get out. He'll almost certainly head for home, won't you, my possums?"

Just at that moment I picked up the basket. Alias stopped pretending to sleep and started to attack the basket with his claws. Whatever a possums was, it was certainly ferocious.

I took the key and stuffed it in my jeans.

The taxi, a grey Granada, was parked a few yards down the road. It had started to rain again. I wondered if they'd offer me a lift. Some hope.

"Goodbye," Miss Tibberton said brightly. "And thank you *so* much."

"Bye." I looked at Smith's back. "See you."

She pretended not to hear. I wasn't surprised.

I'd only gone a few steps when I realized that I'd forgotten my camera. My bag was in the kitchen, where I'd left it on my way to the graveyard. Swearing under my breath, I turned back. Alias was throwing himself from side to side in the basket, making it bounce against my leg. He was surprisingly heavy.

Smith and Miss Tibberton were still standing on the pavement. They had their backs to me, and seemed to be arguing about something.

"But why *there*?" Smith was saying.

"It's got more big cats than anywhere outside London." Miss Tibberton had her hand on the taxi's door. "Aren't we in a hurry?"

"So? Anyway, shouldn't we call Kellaway or someone first?"

The old woman shook her head. "Not till we've gone fishing."

Miss Tibberton cackled as if she'd made the world's best joke. Then, without seeing me, they climbed into the taxi and drove away.

I stood there on the pavement, with the rain dripping

through my hair and Alias going bananas in his mobile prison. That cackle went round and round my head. And I wondered just what the hell I'd got myself into.

CHAPTER THREE

My sister Judith is pretty devious but I can usually tell when she's up to something. This time it took me about 30 seconds.

When I got home, I poked my head into the lounge. Judith was sitting on the sofa in her dressing-gown, painting her toenails. Her hair was wrapped in a towel.

She looked up and gave me her best imitation of a warm, sisterly smile. "There's some tea in the kitchen, if you want it. And I bought some chocolate biscuits."

I left Alias, still in his basket, in the hall. In the kitchen I poured myself some tea and reached for a biscuit. Next thing I noticed was that the washing-up had been done. While Mum and Dad were away, Judith was doing the cooking and I was meant to be doing the washing-up and the Hoovering. The smile and the tea and the biscuits and the empty sink added up to one thing: Judith wanted to ask me a favour.

She'd just have to wait. I went upstairs to my room and put on a Paul Anders tape while I dried my hair and combed it. My mother would have made me change my clothes but I reckoned it wasn't really worth it – my body heat would soon dry them.

For once I wasn't really listening to the music. I was too busy trying to figure out what was going on at Miss Tibberton's. I was also wondering how I was going to develop and print my film before Wednesday.

There was a tap on the door.

"Chris? Can I come in?"

Judith sat on the bed. She wasn't in a hurry to open

negotiations. After about a minute she said, "I like the music. Who is it?"

"Paul Anders. The last time you heard him you said he sounded like a drowned rat."

I thought of adding that drowned rats couldn't make any sort of noise because they were dead. My sister's not what you'd call a logical thinker. But then drowned rats reminded me of Pseud so I said nothing.

"Is that a cat in the hall?" she asked.

I nodded. "I'm looking after it for a day or two. For . . . for a friend."

I'd expected a battle over this but Judith just looked at her fingernails. She took a deep breath. Here it comes, I thought. I carried on combing my hair, watching her in the mirror.

"Clive phoned," she said in a reverent sort of voice.

"Uh huh."

This was hardly the hottest news of the century. He had been phoning at least once a day for the last two months. It drives my dad up the wall because he doesn't like Clive. Clive hasn't got a job, he drives a beat-up 3-litre Capri and he always seems to have loads of money. I'd say they were points in his favour but Dad doesn't see it that way.

Judith cleared her throat. "He asked me to a party. Tonight."

I wished someone had asked me to a party. Preferably someone like Dawn Fisher. She's in our year at school but she doesn't mix with boys who aren't at least two years older than her.

"You don't mind if I go?" Judith said casually. "Would you be all right?"

I shrugged. Of course I'd be all right. What she was really asking me was not to tell Mum and Dad. They'd made her promise to keep an eye on me while they were in Spain.

Judith took a little mirror out of the pocket of her

dressing-gown and began to examine her face, pore by pore. She has a horror of blackheads.

"The thing is," she went on, "it's going to be quite a long party."

I got the picture. She wanted to spend the night with Clive. No wonder she'd done the washing-up. Mum and Dad would explode if they heard.

"All-night rave-up, is it?" I said.

Her mouth tightened, and I thought she was going to snap at me. Just in time she remembered she was asking me a favour.

"In fact it goes on till Monday," she said. "You could call it a sort of marathon party."

To me it sounded more like an old-fashioned dirty weekend. I stuck the comb in my back pocket and turned to face her.

"I'll see you Monday, then," I said. "Have a good time."

"I . . . I can't leave you here alone. I wondered if there was someone you could stay with. You know, a friend."

"Well, there isn't. Everyone's away."

"What about Barry?"

"What about him? He's not exactly a friend."

I don't know what Barry is. He hangs around with us but he's not quite one of us, if you know what I mean. He tries too hard.

"He's always asking you over. I'm sure they'd put you up. They've got lots of room." Before she met Clive, Judith used to go out with Barry's elder brother so she knew the family. I could see she had it all worked out. "His mum would love to have you."

"Yes, but I don't *want* to."

Judith pulled a ten-pound note out of her dressing-gown pocket. "Would that make you want to?"

I shook my head.

She pulled out another ten-pound note and raised her eyebrows.

24

I shrugged.

"It's all I can spare," she said.

I was pretty sure she was telling the truth. It wasn't worth haggling any longer. Besides, if I didn't let her go, she'd make my life hell for the next few days. But I wished she'd just let me stay at home.

"Okay."

"Thanks." She stood up and held out the money. "You'll ring him now?"

"Don't fuss." I took one of the notes. "That's all I need."

"Go on, take it," she said. She sounded irritable, like people often do when you won't let them be generous.

I shook my head and she dropped the second tenner on the bed. Conscience money, I guess. When she left the room, I stuffed both notes into my pocket. I could always use a bit of extra cash.

"Great!" said Barry when I asked him if I could come to stay for a couple of nights; I didn't tell him why. "It'll be brilliant. I'll just go and check with my mother."

He was gone for two or three minutes. I spent them having second thoughts. Barry Sinclair used to live next door to us. That's why everyone, including our parents and Barry himself, assumes we must be friends. Later, when Mr Sinclair got the drugstore franchise, his parents were too grand for a mere council estate and moved to what Barry calls a "des res" in a leafy suburb.

Every week, Barry goes round the estate agents in the area and works out how much the des res is worth. It's an old semi that's been tarted up with a ground-floor extension, gold-plated taps and a patio with a built-in barbecue. Barry says it's becoming quite a major asset.

"Chris?" Barry said in my ear. "You couldn't make it tomorrow, could you? My dad's got some business contacts coming round for a barbecue, and Mum says they're going to spend the night."

Barry lowered his voice respectfully when he said "business contacts". I hoped the barbecue would be rained off.

Aloud I said, "Sure, that's fine." Judith would have to lump it.

"Great! Hey, do you want to go for a swim in the morning? We could meet at the sports centre."

"Okay." I couldn't think of anything better to do. "What time?"

"When it opens? It'll get really crowded later on. And afterwards we can go on to my place."

"Right. I'll see you."

"Hey, wait. Do you want to buy some— ?"

"No," I said automatically.

I almost laughed. No conversation with Barry is complete without him trying to sell you something or buy something from you. When our English teacher asked us what we were going to be, Barry said, quite seriously, that he was going to be a millionaire by the time he was thirty. And I've a horrible feeling that he will.

"We'll talk about it later," Barry said. "See you tomorrow. It'll be great."

Judith wasn't too pleased that I couldn't go to Barry's until the next day. For a moment I thought her responsibilities as a Big Sister were going to come between her and Clive. But I needn't have worried.

Clive called for her at about seven o'clock. I hardly recognized Judith when she came downstairs. She was all high heels and long legs and curves. Didn't look like my sister at all. They could probably smell her perfume on the other side of the river. My father would have had a fit if he'd been here to see her.

Judith hung around for a moment, telling me for

the third time how to lock up properly. Then at last she was gone. I'd been looking forward to being alone. But when she'd left, the house seemed empty, even with Paul Anders blasting out of the stereo system. Alias, who'd been sleeping on the sofa in the lounge, suddenly woke up and decided it was time for supper.

I fed him in the kitchen. I heated up a jumbo packet of oven chips and ate them with tomato ketchup. Alias did something rather disgusting in his cat litter and went to sleep beside the central-heating boiler.

Back in the lounge I tried the TV but all the channels had the usual Bank Holiday rubbish. I wondered what my mates were doing, and whether any of them were having such a boring Saturday night as I was. I wondered why Smith called herself Smith – a damn silly first name for anyone, let alone a girl. Kind of pretentious. I wondered why she thought she was God's gift to the human race. Dawn thinks the same about herself but at least she's got some justification.

The evening was going rapidly downhill. The next thing I thought about was the film I hadn't been able to develop. Barring a miracle, I wouldn't even be able to enter the competition, let alone win it. Between them, Miss Tibberton and Smith had ruined my chances.

Something hard in my pocket was digging into my thigh. I dug my hand in and pulled out the key to Miss Tibberton's flat.

Well, why not? I had a key. No one would be there. I could do it tomorrow. If I replaced the chemicals and paper I used and cleaned up properly, Miss Tibberton wouldn't even know I'd been in her darkroom. If she'd had any decency she'd have suggested the idea herself.

I'd never actually developed and printed a film completely by myself – in the past, there'd always been someone to ask if I hit a snag. This time there wouldn't be any snags.

I went into the kitchen for a pad and a pen and

started making a list of the things I'd need. I had a vague feeling that something was missing. A moment later I realized what it was: Alias was no longer bedded down by the boiler.

I threw down the pen and went to look for him. He was nowhere in the house. I even banged the fork against the open tin of Whiskas to make absolutely sure.

But the kitchen window was open. Just a crack – not enough for a person to get through, but maybe room for a determined cat. Feeling like Sherlock Holmes, I examined the windowsill. Sure enough, I found a tiny piece of something that the trained mind (and nose) identified as used cat litter.

I was tempted to let him go. I hate cats. Then I thought of Miss Tibberton and Pseud's grave. She only had one left.

Five minutes later I was out in the rain once more. I ran most of the way, which isn't much fun when you're carrying a cat basket. I kept my eyes open, of course, especially as I drew nearer to Endymion Street. I remember thinking it was too early for trouble. Things would warm up after closing-time. How stupid can you get.

At last I reached Miss Tibberton's flat. There was a light in one window of the top flat but apart from that the whole house was in darkness. I let myself in and pulled the door shut behind me. It was a Yale, so it locked automatically.

The flat smelled musty, as though no one had lived there for years; it also smelled of cats – oddly enough, I'd never noticed that before. I didn't turn the light on in the hall. There was a street lamp outside so I could see quite well. Even in Endymion Street there might be a nosy, public-spirited neighbour who knew that Miss Tibberton had gone away.

"Alias?" I whispered. "Kitty, kitty, kitty?"

No answer. I fumbled my way down the hall to the

kitchen. When I was inside I closed the door and switched on the light. First thing I saw was Alias, who was crouching under the table and looking meaningfully at his empty bowl.

He glanced at me. For once my reactions were faster than his. I dropped the basket and dived for the cat flap in the back door. I shot the bolt across just before he reached it.

It took me all of ten minutes to get him back in the basket. I was bleeding in three places before I'd finished. I lifted the basket on to the table and stared at him through the bars.

"You belong in a zoo," I snarled.

I washed the scratches under the tap and decided to have a look in the darkroom – a sort of reconnaissance before the big push tomorrow. The darkroom, of course, was really the bathroom, but even Miss Tibberton never called it that. I pushed open the door and switched on the light. My mouth fell open.

No one was going to develop a film or have a bath in there in the immediate future. The black roller blind had been ripped off the window frame. It looked like someone had taken an axe to the enlarger; what was left of it was in the bath. So were the plastic trays for developer, fixer and so on. A whole load of chemicals had been tossed on top, along with stacks of negatives, which must have come from the filing cabinet in the living room. I could also see the remains of two cameras and at least half a dozen lenses.

I felt sick. Physically sick. The rest of the flat was bad enough but nothing had prepared me for this. The destruction in here was in a different league altogether. It was such a waste. It was vicious. I just didn't want to think of how Miss Tibberton must have felt when she found it. More than anything I wanted to be somewhere else.

All this and Pseud? With a .22 bullet in his head?

There had to be a connection. It looked like someone was trying to scare the living daylights out of Miss Tibberton. But why?

I switched off the light and backed out of the room. In the kitchen I picked up the basket, turned off the light and opened the door to the hall. From where I stood I could see the window of the living room. Suddenly I stopped.

Something was moving in the area. A man peered in. The lamplight from the road made him into a black silhouette, rimmed with yellow.

It was so quiet. No traffic passing up the road. Even Alias was silent.

Apart from my own breathing, the only sound was the scrape of a key in the front door.

CHAPTER FOUR

They caught me by the back door.

I was fumbling with the bolts and I didn't even see them. Footsteps thudded on the floor. It sounded like a small army was invading the flat. The kitchen light came on.

Something lifted me up and flung me on to the floor. That was bad. Something landed on my back with a force that drove the air out of my lungs. That was worse. And something hauled my right arm up to my shoulder and gave it an extra yank for luck. That was worst of all.

I yelled. It felt like my arm was broken or my shoulder dislocated or most probably both. A hand snaked round and covered my mouth. The hand smelled of nicotine. I bit it.

Well, that was a mistake. For a long time afterwards I couldn't make any sound at all. I couldn't even breathe because my mouth and nose were covered. While I thrashed around on the floor I was vaguely aware that they were searching me. By that I mean they made quite sure that I wasn't carrying a weapon the size of a penny anywhere on my person. Finally they let me go. I stayed in a huddle on the kitchen floor. I didn't want to get up.

"Up you get."

It was a man's voice, and it sounded like it was used to giving orders. I rolled over and managed to sit up. There was blood on my face and in my mouth. It tasted salty. One of my front teeth had lost a corner.

Three men were in the room, which seemed to have shrunk since I last saw it. I focused on the nearest of them. He was well over six feet and broad to match.

He wore a dripping raincoat, and he had his hands deep in the pockets. Maybe one of the hands was decorated with my teethmarks. He had big eyes, a big nose and an unexpectedly small mouth that was shut very tightly. His collar was too tight for his thick, bulging neck. I guessed he was in his thirties.

"How did you get in?" he said.

"I've got a key," I mumbled. I couldn't see any point in lying. "Miss Tibberton gave it to me."

The man turned aside and poked through the pile of my belongings on the table. "Check it," he said.

A younger bloke in a dark-green anorak picked up the key and went into the hall. I could hear him trying it in the front door.

I was trembling. I guessed these must be the same people who'd been here before.

Green Anorak came back. He had a round, freckled face, in the middle of which was a sharp little nose like a bird's beak.

"It fits, sir," he said.

The big man produced a card encased in plastic and waved it under my nose for about two seconds. There was a photo on it, plus some writing. He didn't give me time to read the words or look at the picture.

"Detective Inspector Gryson," he said. "Your name? Address?"

Police? I felt a rush of relief. Then I realized that these blokes weren't friendly neighbourhood bobbies, and most of the relief ebbed away.

I told him what he wanted to know. The third bloke, who was leaning against the sink, scribbled it all down in his notebook. He did it automatically – you could tell that the three of them were used to working as a team.

Green Anorak bent down and peered at Alias, who spat at him. Green Anorak kicked the cat basket halfway across the kitchen. Gryson didn't even turn round.

"Phone number?"

32

When I told him, he didn't take my word for it. Miss Tibberton's phone was in the kitchen, along with the directories. He dug out A-D and looked up my dad's entry. While Gryson was doing that, Green Anorak wandered around the flat, opening doors and rifling through cupboards. Things were chaotic to begin with, but he made them worse. A plate with a flowered pattern smashed on the floor. He just left the pieces lying there. He struck me as the sort of guy who takes a pleasure in his work.

But how did the police fit into this? Maybe Miss Tibberton had reported what had happened earlier.

"Where's Miss Tibberton?" Gryson said, blowing my theory.

"She's gone away."

"Where?"

"She didn't say."

"For how long?"

"A few days. She didn't know when she'd be back."

"And why are you here?"

"I'm looking after her cat. I took him home but he came back here, so I had to fetch him. Nothing wrong in that, is there?"

"I ask the questions." Gryson moved a step nearer. "Get it?"

I nodded. My arm was still throbbing.

"Take a look in here," Green Anorak interrupted. He'd opened the door to the bathroom.

Gryson glanced over his shoulder. He didn't seem surprised to see the mess, but I don't think he was expecting it, either. He went in and had a good look. Then he turned to me.

"You do that?"

"Of course not."

Gryson came back into the kitchen and stared thoughtfully at me. "But you knew about it, didn't you?"

"I saw it just now." I was telling the truth but I

33

knew I sounded guilty. I even felt myself blushing.

"When did you last see Miss Tibberton?"

"This afternoon."

I was still as scared as hell but I was also getting mad. I wasn't stupid enough to show it, of course. Gryson was treating me like some kind of criminal and that made me bloody-minded. Then something struck me that made me wonder if they really were police after all. All I had was Gryson's word for it. They'd used a key to open the front door. Where had they got it from? It didn't seem likely that Miss Tibberton had given it to them. And it certainly didn't sound as if she'd asked them to have a look round in her absence. Green Anorak was handling her possessions like he was a human bulldozer. And they hadn't exactly been gentle with me.

The Inspector – if that's what he was – carried on with the questions. After a bit they began to go round in circles. I didn't tell him any lies but I didn't go out of my way to deluge him with information. It took him quite a while to dig out the details of how I'd met Miss Tibberton at the evening class. And some things I didn't get round to mentioning at all, like Smith and what had happened to Pseud and the snatches of conversation I'd overheard this afternoon. At that point I wasn't intentionally holding out on Gryson. It was just that I didn't see why I should go out of my way to be helpful.

I don't know how long it went on. It seemed like hours but it was probably only about ten minutes.

Suddenly Gryson changed tack and asked a question he hadn't tried before: "You ever meet anyone else here? This afternoon, especially?"

Something in his tone had changed. This was the question he'd been wanting to ask all along. For some reason I remembered how Smith had looked. Angry? Arrogant? Pale, yes, and maybe scared. I opened my mouth before I knew what I was going to say.

"Well?" he snapped. "Did you? A girl, maybe? About your age?"

The doorbell rang.

It was a stupid, homely sound, and it gave us all a shock. Gryson muttered something that sounded like "I knew it!" The other two were suddenly about five times more alert than they had been before. As for me, I was relieved to have a breathing space.

Green Anorak went to answer the door. A few seconds later a woman was standing in the doorway of the kitchen. Her short, fair hair glistened with rain. She had a bony face that reminded me of an intelligent horse.

She frowned at me and said, in the sort of voice that can freeze water in ten seconds, "Good evening, Gryson."

Gryson took a step backwards and tried the effect of a smile. The woman was younger than him and about half his weight; but she obviously scared him rigid.

"Good evening, madam." Even his voice had changed. He'd soaked his vocal cords in castor oil since he last spoke. "We weren't sure whether to expect you."

The woman jerked her head at him. Gryson followed her out of the kitchen. Green Anorak folded his arms and glanced at his colleague, who closed his notebook with a snap. Then there was silence, broken only by the ticking of the electric clock on the wall and the patter of the rain on the window.

I was still sitting on the floor, my arms round my knees. If the woman was Gryson's boss, what would that make her? A Chief Inspector? A Superintendent? She seemed surprisingly young for that sort of rank but maybe the CID were going in for accelerated promotion these days. To be honest, I didn't really care: all I wanted to know was whether she'd let me go home.

The breathing space was useful. For the first time since Gryson started putting the boot in, I had a chance to think about what was happening. Assuming they *were*

35

police, I didn't think they would arrest me, because they would have done that already; and even if they did, Miss Tibberton would clear me when they found her. I reckoned they weren't the same people as the ones who vandalized the flat and killed Pseud: the bathroom had come as a genuine surprise to them. On the other hand, they didn't behave like police are meant to behave. I don't enjoy being treated like Public Enemy Number One, especially when I happen to be innocent. And I had a strong suspicion that they weren't protecting Miss Tibberton – they were hunting her.

The only certainty I had was that Miss Tibberton was getting a raw deal somewhere along the line, and that didn't seem fair. Besides which, I owed her – partly for all the times she'd let me use her darkroom, and partly for the three occasions when she'd looked at one of my photographs and said in a grudging voice, "That's not bad".

There were footsteps in the hall. The front door slammed. Then Gryson was in the kitchen again.

"Where were we?" he said to no one in particular.

Number 3 opened his notebook. "You were asking Dalham if he'd ever seen anyone here. Particularly this afternoon."

Gryson nodded and turned to me. "Well? Have you?"

I'm a good liar. Our history teacher says it's one of the few social skills I have. I just shook my head.

"Never?" The rasp was back in Gryson's voice but it wasn't quite as menacing as before. Maybe his superior had given him a bollocking for roughing up a suspect. "You've been here maybe a dozen times and you've never met anyone?"

"That's right."

Don't make it complicated – that's my advice if you have to start lying. Keep it simple and keep it as close to the truth as you can. And it was almost the truth. The only person I'd ever met at Miss Tibberton's was the girl named Smith. I didn't owe her anything. For all I cared, Gryson could have her for breakfast. But I had a feeling that if I mentioned her to him, Miss Tibberton would be the one who'd suffer.

"Not this afternoon? Sure?"

I shook my head again.

"All right. We may be in touch, so I don't want you leaving home for the next few days. Understand?"

I swallowed. "You mean I can go?"

"That's right. On your bike."

I scrambled up. Gryson gestured at the little heap of my possessions on the table. I stuffed them in my pockets – everything except Miss Tibberton's key. Gryson put his hand on it when I tried to pick it up. I wasn't arguing. He was welcome to it.

I guess the relief I was feeling must have showed on my face, because Green Anorak grinned unexpectedly as he opened the kitchen door for me.

"Wait a minute," Gryson said behind me.

I turned back. My stomach did a somersault. Suddenly I knew what they were up to. Pretending to let me go was just an interrogation technique to soften me up. No wonder Green Anorak smiled.

Gryson wasn't smiling. His face looked like he'd swallowed half a lemon. "Aren't you forgetting something?"

"What?"

"That bloody cat."

CHAPTER FIVE

I was about halfway home when I realized that someone was following me.

At first I'd been so relieved to get out of the flat that I'd hardly noticed where I was going. I wanted to run, but after the first few yards Alias and the cat basket slowed me to a fast walk. I barely noticed where I was going – just trusted to autopilot to get me back. My head was buzzing, and I was panting and feeling slightly sick as though I'd just run a race and come last. For once I didn't keep my eyes on the other people in Endymion Street.

But one of them must have had his eyes on me.

The lights and bustle of the High Road woke me up. It was later than I'd thought, and people were already beginning to come out of the pubs. A gang of teenagers were running towards me, filling the width of the pavement. Most of them weren't much older than me. They were yelling and generally mucking about. One of them chucked a beer can at a bus. He missed.

All in all, they were probably harmless, but I wasn't in the mood for taking chances. Besides, I couldn't run far with Alias's basket and the basket itself was just the sort of thing that would make them curious. So I slipped into a side road.

I've known this area since I was a kid so I knew exactly where I was. If I zigzagged across it, I'd avoid the main roads for most of the way home. It would take a little longer but it would be much easier on the nerves.

The further I got from the High Road, the quieter it got. The streets were mainly residential and they were beginning to come up in the world. But they still had a long

38

way to go: none of the houses was what Barry would have called a des res. I met a few people on their way home or walking dogs. The rain slackened off to a drizzle. Finally it stopped altogether.

The streetlights were playing tricks with the puddles and the rain made everything glisten as though it had been varnished. By now I'd calmed down a bit. I found myself thinking about the possibilities of night photography. But to get halfway decent results you need the right equipment. £500 would barely cover the essentials. And I wasn't even in line for that competition any more.

I stopped for a moment, to shift the basket from one hand to the other. One of my shoelaces was undone so I tied it up. It was sopping wet.

It was then that I began to get worried. I'd heard, without really registering, the sound of footsteps some way behind me: they went *soft – loud – soft – loud*, as if the bloke had a drawing-pin in the heel of one shoe but not in the other. But when I stopped, the footsteps stopped too, and I noticed the sudden silence. And when I moved off they started again.

There didn't have to be a connection. You get a lot of weirdos on the streets at night. Then I thought that maybe one of Gryson's men was checking that I really was going home. There was one more possibility, and that was the one I liked least of all: whoever killed Pseud and smashed up the flat could be on my tail.

I tried the usual tricks, like they do on TV. I sneaked a glance behind me when I turned the next corner. There was no one in sight, but the footsteps stopped. Then I went on turning right until I'd done four sides of a square. The footsteps followed me round.

That clinched it. For a few minutes I just carried on walking, hardly noticing where I was going. I thought about ringing the nearest doorbell and asking for help, or trying to make a run for it. Then Alias's basket jarred against a row of iron railings and I had a better idea.

Just round the next corner there was a break in the railings. I dived through and ran clumsily into the belt of trees that lined one side of the little park. It was surprisingly dark once I'd got there. I reckoned that was in my favour. It was unlikely that the bloke behind me knew the layout as well as I did.

On the far side of the trees was a high brick wall with people's gardens beyond it. A muddy path ran between the trees and wall. Years ago we used to use the path for dirt-track racing on our bikes until a group of local residents got overheated about it. I walked along it as quietly as I could, listening for the sounds of someone coming through the trees. No one did.

The wall gave way to a much lower wooden fence. A section of the fence had rotted away and been plugged with rusting chicken wire. You used to be able to pull up one corner and slip through. You still could.

I pushed the basket through the hole and then slid through myself. I pulled the chicken wire back. Alias miaowed as if his heart was breaking and I nearly killed him on the spot.

I was at one end of a row of allotments that backed on to the railway. A train came by. The people sitting in the safe, brightly-lit carriages were living in another world.

It was too dark to see much, so I just started walking. The earth was wet and heavy. God knows how many lettuces and stuff I trampled on. My shoes squelched softly at every step. I kept stumbling over plants and once I nearly sprained my ankle. The only consolation was that anyone behind me would be making just as much noise.

A few minutes later I climbed over the wall that marked the opposite boundary of the allotments. I had to drop the basket from the top, and Alias didn't like it. You'd think I'd broken every bone in his body by the noise he made. No one saw us coming into the cul-de-sac on the other side. A police car cruised along the road at the mouth of the cul-de-sac but it didn't stop.

We went the rest of the way along well-lit main roads. It was like one of those journeys in a nightmare, when you know everything would be okay if only you could reach your destination, but you never do.

As far as I knew, no one was behind me. But I wasn't sure. That was like a nightmare, too.

Well, what do you do when you come home to an empty house?

You're tired, wet, muddy and most of all scared. You've been beaten up, questioned and chased. You don't know what the hell's going on.

I'll tell you what you do. You shut the kitchen window. You feed the cat. Alias, the cause of all the trouble, was behaving as if nothing had happened: he was hungry, and that was the only thing that mattered.

Afterwards I had a bath, found some clean clothes and made some tea with a lot of sugar in it. Then I sat in the sitting room, with Alias purring dementedly on my knee, and stared at the phone. The phone didn't have any answers, either.

I couldn't phone Judith, even if she and Clive were in, because British Telecom and Clive had had a disagreement over the quarterly bill. Anyway, Judith is never any good in a crisis, and her ego's big enough for two already without me asking her for help. Maybe I could have talked to my parents about it – or maybe not. But they were in Spain, so that was that.

I just wanted to talk to someone – to see what the reaction was. Preferably someone who was already involved, which in this case meant Miss Tibberton. Or the American girl who obviously thought I was some sort of household pest, like bedbugs or cockroaches. It shows you how low I was: if I could have phoned Smith, I'd have done it.

There was so little to go on. All I knew for sure was that someone had it in for Miss Tibberton, and that she'd probably run away from them. And Gryson wanted to find her, too. I had an idea where she might be, but if she'd wanted the police to know where she was, she'd have told them herself. Come to that, she would have reported the break-in and Pseud's murder. So – either the police and Miss Tibberton were on opposite sides of the fence, or Gryson wasn't really a policeman.

I pushed Alias away and found the number for divisional headquarters in the phone book. I was sure there was no way they could trace the call. While the phone rang I fought the temptation to put down the receiver. On the ninth ring it was answered by the sergeant on duty.

"Can I speak to Detective Inspector Gryson?" I said in the deepest voice I could manage.

"Who?"

I repeated the name.

"Never heard of him," the sergeant said in a bored voice. "You sure he works here?"

"I don't know. I think so."

"There're no Grysons in CID, son. You can take my word for it. Look, what's this all about?"

"I want to report a burglary." I took a deep breath. "There . . . there were three men, and one of them called himself Detective Inspector Gryson."

"They said they were police?"

"Yeah."

"I see. Go on."

I guessed by his tone he didn't believe me. I suppose he has to deal with a lot of nutters on a Saturday night.

"They were in the bottom flat of 85 Endymion Street. Where Miss Tibberton lives. It was about an hour ago I— "

"What's that address?" the sergeant snapped. Suddenly he didn't sound bored.

I told him again.

There was a short silence. I could hear paper rustling at the other end of the line, the ringing of another phone and the clatter of a typewriter. Then the sergeant cleared his throat.

"I think we got a crossed wire there, son. *Gryson*, you say? I thought you said Grey. That's fine – it's all under control. We know all about that. Nothing to worry about." The sergeant sounded very worried indeed. "Now, just for the record, can you tell me your name and address?"

Something was wrong, I was sure. I hadn't found any answers – just a lot more questions.

"Smith," I heard myself say. "Clive Smith." I'd somehow made a decision without being conscious of it. "And I live at 88 Endymion Street."

Then I put the phone down.

CHAPTER SIX

"Hey, Chris!" Barry said. "Great to see you."

"Hi." In the circumstances I thought I'd be polite, so I unhitched the headphones of the Walkman and added: "How're you doing?"

"Great!" Barry blinked at the cat basket. "What's that?"

"It's a cat basket," I said.

He frowned and took a step sideways so he could peer into it. Alias, who'd had one and a half tins of Whiskas for breakfast, was just a pulsating lump of ginger fur.

"That's a cat," Barry told me, presumably in case I thought it was a red squirrel or a tiger cub. "Why've you brought it here?"

I avoided the question and concentrated on giving Alias a good character reference: "He's very quiet – spends most of his time asleep. Just needs feeding now and then."

"Since when have you had a cat?"

"Since yesterday afternoon."

I was in the entrance hall of the sports centre, sitting on the floor with my back against the wall. Beside me was a big carrier bag that contained Alias's belongings and a change of clothes for me. Sunlight streamed through the windows and poured itself into puddles on the carpet. I was in one of the puddles, and it was making me feel sleepy. Yesterday's rain belonged to yesterday.

Barry sat down beside me. He's a bit smaller than me and when I look at his face my spot problem doesn't seem quite as bad as usual. His skin has got quite a lot in common with an erupting volcano.

44

Today he was wearing his new leather jacket, the one that should have cost over £150; it didn't, because his father knows a man who knows a man who can get leather jackets for even less than cost price. Underneath the jacket he wore a Paul Anders T-shirt. I should be flattered: he only bought it because I've got one.

"We can't take a cat swimming, Chris," he explained patiently. "They probably wouldn't even let us in. I mean, he's livestock, isn't he? There's a byelaw about livestock."

Barry knows a lot about byelaws. I could see he was about to tell me most of what he knew there and then if I didn't stop him. There was only one sure way to do that.

"Do you want to earn some money?" I said.

Instantly a sort of glazed look came into his eyes. "How much and what for?"

"There's something I've got to do today. I just want you to look after the cat till tonight."

"But we're going swimming today. Then we're going back to my place."

"Something's come up," I said. "I can't come over till this evening. But in the meantime, I'd like you to look after Alias."

"Who?"

"That's the cat's name. Your mum won't mind if I'm late, will she?"

Barry shook his head – absentmindedly, as if the question was hardly worth asking or answering. Mrs Sinclair's amazingly easy-going. She just moons around with a smile on her face and does whatever Barry and his dad want. Totally unlike my mother.

"But why?" he asked. "What've you got to do?"

I shrugged and looked mysterious.

"Come on. You can tell me."

I knew from Barry's tone that telling him what I was up to was going to be part of the deal. Which meant telling him a lie, or at least sending his imagination off on a false scent.

"I've got to see someone."

"Male or female?"

"Female."

"A girl?" Barry tried to keep his voice casual. "You got a girl?"

I nodded, and the truth changed to a lie. I knew that Barry wanted a girlfriend almost as much as he wanted to be a millionaire.

"That's nice. Anyone I know?"

"I don't think so."

"Good-looking, is she?"

"I've seen worse." As I spoke I thought of Smith and I nearly laughed out loud. "Kind of special."

"It's not Dawn Fisher, is it?" Barry asked suspiciously. Like everyone else, he has fantasies about Dawn.

"Of course it isn't." I decided to turn the screw a bit. "She's got a bit more class than that. In fact she's American."

I knew I shouldn't have told him that. It just slipped out because Smith was in my mind for reasons that had nothing to do with romance.

I refused to tell him any more, except that no one else knew about it yet. I swore him to secrecy. That made him feel good because he likes knowing things that no one else does. Then we got down to the part that Barry really enjoyed: the haggling.

"How much were you thinking of?" he asked.

I shrugged. "You won't have to do anything except carry him home. It's only a cat. How about two quid?"

Barry shook his head sadly. "We're talking about a totally ruined day. I can't go swimming. I won't be able to do anything. It'll mean an argument with my mum —"

"I thought she did whatever you wanted."

"She doesn't like cats. Anyway, she's in a right state this morning because my dad's deal fell through last night and he blamed it on the food she bought for the barbecue. The steaks were tough. And it rained."

"Well, that wasn't her fault."

"The point is," Barry went on, "Dad wants to sublet the flat above his shop and he thought he had it all fixed up with these two contacts of his, and . . ."

He droned on for about five minutes, telling me exactly why he thought the deal fell through. I stopped listening after about thirty seconds. He finds these things fascinating. I had no idea why he had to tell me all about it, unless it was one of the less obvious parts of his bargaining technique, like almost everything else he says. The collapse of the deal meant his dad was in a foul temper, which meant his mum was on the verge of a nervous breakdown, which meant that Barry would have to soften her up with a bunch of flowers before he introduced Alias into the house. And so on.

At last he got to the point: ". . . So I couldn't possibly do it for less than a tenner. You do see that?"

"Ten quid!" I almost lost my temper. "For keeping an eye on a cat? Just for a few hours? You're joking."

But he wasn't. He thought he had me over a barrel, and in a way he was right. I put in a counter-offer. He held firm and we argued some more. Then he got up, sighed theatrically and started to walk away.

"Barry. Wait."

In fact he'd already stopped. I put down a five pound note and three pound coins on the floor. "Deal?" I said. "It's my last offer."

"Okay." Barry scooped up the money. "You know something, Chris? You drive a hard bargain. I respect that."

The coach was full of children.

They were eating crisps and swilling fizzy drinks. They were climbing over the seatbacks and screaming. They were running up and down the aisle and being sick from the sheer excitement. I hate kids.

I had a window seat, which I'd been lucky to get at such short notice. I spent most of the two-and-a-half hour journey staring at the traffic on the motorway. There were the usual Bank Holiday roadworks and the usual Bank Holiday traffic jams. I insulated myself from the racket with Paul Anders at full blast. After a few minutes, the woman in the next seat had the nerve to nudge me and ask me to turn the volume down. I ask you. Her children were shrieking blue murder in the seats across the aisle.

We reached the city about midday. The coach vomited out its passengers at the bus station near the main shopping centre. Most people seemed to be heading for the new entertainments complex or visiting relatives.

I had a rough idea of the geography. A few years back, we had spent a fortnight at Easton, which is a seaside resort a few miles away; we used to come here quite a lot. There was a town map at the bus station, and I checked my route before I set off.

It was a long, hot walk, most of it uphill. I passed the cathedral, the university and endless shops and offices. Then there were lots of old houses laid out in squares and crescents and avenues – all very des res. Then the ground levelled out. The zoo was up here, along with a church, several hotels and a mini-stately home in a fancy garden. On the other side of the road was a big common, part of which had been taken over by a funfair.

I turned left, in the direction of the zoo and the funfair. I was starving, and my throat felt like a sponge that had been baked in an oven. There was an ice cream van parked in a lay-by. I looked at my watch. A few minutes' delay wouldn't make any difference: either they'd be there or they wouldn't.

I joined the queue and finally bought the largest cone they sold, stuffed with chocolate flakes. I moved away towards the zoo, gobbling the ice cream and trying to stuff the change into my jeans. A coin missed the pocket and

48

clattered on the pavement. I swung round and stooped to pick it up.

As I straightened up, I happened to glance across the road. A green Rover was parked on a double-yellow line. I think there were two people inside, both in the front. The driver raised a newspaper to shield his face. But he was a fraction of a second too slow.

It was too hot for him to be wearing the green anorak. But he couldn't do much to change that round, freckled face with the pointy little nose like the beak of a bird.

The ice cream nearly fell out of my hand. I just couldn't believe what had happened.

When you get a shock like that, you react at once: the thinking comes afterwards. In a daze, I carried on walking in the same direction as before. I even swallowed a mouthful of chocolate flake. Five seconds later I realized it was about the best thing I could have done. By now, Green Anorak must be reasonably sure I hadn't seen him. As far as he was concerned, I was carrying on as normal.

My brain started functioning again, after a fashion. They must have followed me here, all the way down from London. They must have guessed that I'd try to warn Miss Tibberton. When I lost whoever was following me home last night, they simply picked up the trail again when I left the house this morning.

The main entrance to the zoo was on my right. That was the one place I had to avoid. The car park at the front was packed and people were pouring through the turnstiles. I walked on.

At least two of them, and in a car. I needed to find somewhere with a lot of exits and where you couldn't take cars. I looked across the road. I needed the funfair.

There was a zebra crossing fifty yards away, so I headed for that. Just before I reached it, a group of people surged across the road from the side where the funfair was. When the group reached the pavement, it broke up like a wave when it hits the shore. Two people were coming straight for me. An old woman and a girl with a pale face and dark hair. By now they were only a few yards away from me.

The green Rover coasted across the road, ignoring the oncoming traffic, and pulled up at the crossing.

Smith wasn't looking at the Rover. Her face suddenly flamed with anger. She nudged Miss Tibberton and pointed at me.

Then everything spun out of my control.

CHAPTER SEVEN

"You fool!" Miss Tibberton said.

There wasn't any doubt that she was talking to me. As a matter of fact, she never said anything else to me again.

The two front doors of the Rover opened simultaneously. Green Anorak and a man I didn't recognize scrambled out. The second bloke had red hair and wore this really stupid double-breasted navy-blue blazer with brass buttons.

The pavement was thick with people. I didn't know if Miss Tibberton had even seen the car, let alone realized that the men inside were after her and Smith. Once again, I didn't have time to think about it. I just threw the ice cream instead.

The cornet curved above the heads of the crowd and landed smack on Green Anorak's cheek. It disintegrated. Most of the ice cream either fell directly to the ground or slid there more slowly, leaving a white and slimy trail down Green Anorak's face and clothes.

At first he had no idea what had hit him. He let out a screech and scraped frantically at his dripping cheek. He stared wildly around, trying to find out where the ice cream had come from. In other circumstances it might have been funny.

Smith reacted faster than Miss Tibberton. Her eyes followed where the ice cream went. She must have put two and two together at the speed of light because she grabbed Miss Tibberton's arm and pulled her through the crowd, away from the Rover and away from me.

In a way, the crowd was a godsend. There were people

51

milling along the pavement in both directions, people waiting to go over the crossing, and of course the group that had just come over from the other side. It was thickest where the Rover was.

Green Anorak started to push his way through – not after me, but after Miss Tibberton and Smith. It just wasn't his day. He tried to muscle between two big blokes. They started shouting. He started shouting.

"Who d'you think you are?" the larger of the men said. He was wearing jeans, boots and nothing else except a few tattoos.

"Police," Green Anorak said, still trying to push through. "Get out of my way."

They were talking at the top of their voices, so everyone within a thirty-yard radius was eavesdropping.

"Who are you pushing around?" The bloke put a massive hand on Green Anorak's chest and shoved him into the road.

Green Anorak bounced back. By this time his mate had come round the car. They joined forces and charged. There was a blur of arms and legs, and a lot of swearing. I couldn't see exactly what happened because people were blocking my view. Then Green Anorak and his friend were past the worst of the crowd and the two men were writhing on the pavement. The crowd was oohing and ahing but none of them even tried to intervene. Someone was having hysterics, and an elderly gent said loudly that one could never find a policeman when one wanted one. Obviously he didn't believe Green Anorak, either. That made two of us. There was quite a bit of blood, probably from someone's nose.

I backed away. They were after Miss Tibberton and Smith, not me. There was nothing I could do to help. It was time to look after Number One, which meant making myself scarce as quickly as possible.

Not very heroic, eh? You think I should have galloped off on my white horse and rescued Miss Tibberton and

Smith? Well, I didn't have a white horse and it wasn't my quarrel in the first place. Besides, I'd seen what had happened to the two blokes and I didn't want it to happen to me. It's all very well seeing that sort of thing on a TV screen, but in real life it sort of turns your stomach.

I won't pretend I wasn't a little ashamed, but that's my affair. I sidled back the way I'd come, glancing over my shoulder because I was still as curious as hell. I was moving uphill so I had quite a good view over the heads of the crowd. I nearly said "the audience", not "the crowd", because an audience was just what they were. I bet that most of them enjoyed the whole thing. I'm surprised they didn't start clapping.

The first time I turned round, Miss Tibberton and Smith were still running, and Green Anorak and Partner, though hampered by the crowd, had gained on them. The next time I looked, only seconds later, I couldn't believe my eyes. Miss Tibberton and Smith were standing still. As I watched they turned tail and belted *towards* Green Anorak. Then I realized why.

Detective Inspector Gryson was pounding up the hill towards them, waving his arms. He looked like a human tank in full battle order.

Just for a moment, I forgot about running away. It's hard to explain why: what was happening gripped me against my will. It was like when you can't stop watching a horror movie that's scaring you to death but much worse.

The whole scene is fixed in my mind – I couldn't get rid of it if I tried – because of the way it ended.

A car backfired. That's what it sounded like – a *crack!* that for an instant pushed all the other noises into the background.

But it wasn't a car.

Miss Tibberton jerked sideways and fell. Think of a toy soldier flicked over by an invisible small boy. Now you see it, now you don't. The crowd swirled and I couldn't see her. People started to cluster round her like iron filings round a magnet.

But there wasn't time to think about it. Maybe that was just as well.

Smith, after one terrified glance, ran on. Gryson shouted something I couldn't hear. Green Anorak put his head down and charged through the crowd in the general direction of Miss Tibberton. His colleague in the natty blazer tried to catch Smith.

She was smart. She feinted like a footballer round one side of a large woman with three toddlers and a double-barrelled pushchair. GA's colleague bought it. Smith darted round the other side of the woman and was clear. For the moment.

I heard a whistle behind me. A uniformed cop, helmet and all, was flying down the road. I started moving. I didn't know what the hell I was doing. I should have left the whole thing alone and gone and talked to the monkeys or something.

I saw Smith's face when she saw PC Plod. She was scared of him too. A couple of seconds later I was by her side. I grabbed her wrist. It felt thinner, more fragile, than I'd expected. She looked at me – just for an instant – and for the first time I noticed her eyes properly. The mind does choose some stupid times to notice things. Just for the record, the eyes were blue, with sort of greeny flecks in them.

Then we were running again. Over the zebra crossing. I led and Smith followed. It wasn't as easy as it sounds, because the traffic wasn't ready for us. There was a lot of swearing and honking. Drivers are always worse-tempered in hot weather.

We reached the other side and plunged into the funfair, which was like all travelling funfairs, though bigger than most. And it was full to capacity because it was a fine Bank Holiday Sunday.

Smith and I just ran. It was a blur of roundabouts and

dodgems, coconut shies and shooting ranges, grottoes of love and tunnels of horror, fortune tellers and fun houses and halls of mirrors and Helter Skelters and big wheels and Waltzers. There was every machine you could think of, and most of them seemed to be playing a tune or bleeping or roaring. There were millions of people, and almost as many goldfish for the people to win.

I had a stitch but I was too scared to stop. Behind us we left a trail of shouting. It's impossible to run through a crowd without treading on a few toes and we must have trodden on hundreds. Someone started yelling, "Stop, thief!" and "Police!"

I didn't even bother to look back. There wasn't time. Anyway, I knew what I'd see: Gryson and Co., and one of them must have a gun.

The crowd began to thin and I guessed we were nearing the edge of the funfair. A minute later we ran through a line of gigantic diesel trucks and on to the open common. In the confusion of the fair we'd made a right-angled turn and started running parallel to the road rather than away from it. We were a long way past the zoo and the zebra crossing. On the far side of the road was a high stone wall, broken by a pair of wrought-iron gates that were standing open.

I glanced over my shoulder and saw Green Anorak disentangling himself from a man selling hot-air balloons. He was maybe forty yards away. Several of the balloons surged into the air, and the seller was demanding payment. There was no sign of Gryson and the Blazer.

"Come on," I gasped. "Over the road again."

That was easier said than done because there was no place to cross and we had to dive across the stream of traffic. Luckily it was moving quite slowly. When we reached the other side, we looked back. Green Anorak was sprinting towards the road. The man he'd run into was lying on the grass. And dozens of brightly-coloured balloons were climbing into the sky.

I grabbed Smith's hand and pulled her across the crowded pavement and through the gateway. It was like walking into another world. The noise level dropped and there was hardly anyone around. Just miles of thick yew hedges with gravel paths alongside, plus a few flowerbeds with herbs and things growing in them. It was all very formal, like a 3D exercise in geometry. The main drive ran straight up to a redbrick house with lots of tall chimneys.

You remember the mini-stately home I mentioned? I'd been here once before with Judith on one of the Easton holidays, years ago when I was a kid. It was owned by the council or someone. You had to pay to get into the house, which was some sort of museum, but the grounds were free. I didn't go into the house – Judith let me have the money instead. I just mooched around the garden while she went round the place with her nose in the air, pretending she was Lady Muck of the Manor.

We didn't linger to admire the surroundings but zoomed into a long walk with yew hedges, six feet high, on either side. I was still in the lead; I could hear Smith panting behind me. The path ended in a T-junction: we went left. At the next T-junction we went right.

The paths were laid out almost like a maze. I was banking on that, and on the fact that there was another, smaller gate on the far side of the garden. If we could lose Green Anorak for a few minutes and reach the second gate, I reckoned we'd have at least a small hope of getting away.

I careered round another corner. I'd only gone a few yards when I heard a squawk. I glanced back. Smith was no longer there.

So I made a U-turn and went back to the last junction. The hundred-percent hero would have charged round, ready for anything. But I stopped and peered cautiously round the corner of the hedge.

Smith was face down on the gravel, wriggling like a

stranded fish. Green Anorak was also face down, just behind her. It looked as if he'd flung himself forward and grabbed her ankle, bringing them both down. At present he was hauling himself hand over hand up her leg, trying to crush her with his body. It was like he was climbing a rope up the side of a mountain.

Don't ask me how, but I knew that this was my very last chance. My chance to get shot of this business. My chance to slip back to London, lie low in Barry's des res, stuff myself with his mum's three-course meals and pretend that nothing had happened. I didn't know what was happening here. All I knew was that people were getting hurt, badly hurt, and I didn't want me to end up the same way.

Green Anorak was up to Smith's waist by now. Another heave and he'd have done it. Smith was still thrashing around but less violently than before.

She made one last effort and did a sort of press-up, raising her head and shoulders as far as she could. Her eyes met mine. Blue eyes, with sort of greeny flecks in them.

CHAPTER EIGHT

I ran forward and took a running jump on to Green Anorak.

I got lucky. He was just pulling himself up for his final spring and his body had twisted, so I landed on his side just above the waist. God knows what I had in mind – pulling him off by the hair, maybe, or something equally stupid. He was about twice as heavy as me and three or four times as nasty.

Suddenly the situation changed. I lost control of my body and sprawled sideways. Green Anorak curled up on the gravel and yelled with pain.

Smith hauled herself up. I picked myself out of the yew hedge where I'd landed and stared at Green Anorak. I remember wondering if by a hundred-to-one chance I'd got his kidneys. I don't even know where the kidneys are. I had a terrible feeling he might need a doctor. I even glanced round to see if there was anyone we could ask to get help.

"Move!" Smith yelled at me.

The spell broke, and we started running again. We met no one on the way. I kept us close to the wall, and about five minutes later we found the second gate.

On the other side was a quiet, tree-lined road. Most of the parked cars were BMWs or Mercs, and that was at the lower end of the scale; it was the kind of neighbourhood Barry would have approved of. We kept moving, always on side roads and always away from the common. After a while we slowed to a fast walk. Both of us were in poor shape. I thought I was quite fit, but running for your life does take it out of you.

"I need a break," Smith said.

Apart from "Move!", it was the first thing she'd said to me. I don't mind admitting I could have done with a word of appreciation. Just something to show that she recognized I'd done her a favour.

"Where are you staying?" I said. "Can we go there?"

She shook her head. "Miss Tibberton's got the key in her bag. Besides . . ."

"Besides what?"

She shook her head again. I didn't press her. We'd just come into a square that had a public garden in the middle of it. I pointed and set off towards it, hardly caring whether she followed. But she did.

There was an old drinking fountain in the middle of the garden. That water tasted better than any drink I've had, before or since. Afterwards we lay on the grass under a tree near one of the gates. We weren't conspicuous because loads of people were lying around just like us, sunning themselves and talking. Anyway we chose a spot where we couldn't be seen from the road.

I waited for her to speak. Even then I was expecting her to say something like "Thanks" or "Sorry for dragging you into this". But it didn't turn out like that.

She picked a daisy and stared at it as though it contained the Meaning of Life. "You really blew it," she said bitterly. She wasn't talking to the daisy.

Her words were so unexpected that I didn't know what to say. In the end I muttered, "Come again?", which must have sounded pretty feeble.

"We weren't followed last night," she said angrily. "So they must have followed you. How did you know?"

"Where to come? I heard Miss Tibberton say something about more big cats than anywhere else in England. She was always rabbitting on about the zoo here. So I took a chance and came."

"For God's sake, why?" Smith snapped. Then she

waved her hand at me. "It doesn't matter. The damage is done."

I glared at her. "It does matter. To me. I was coming to warn her."

That got her interested. I explained about Alias going back to the flat last night, and about Gryson and Co. roughing me up.

"You didn't tell them about me?" she said quickly. "Or about where we'd come?"

"No. God knows why. And then someone followed me home. So I rang the police."

"You did *what*?" She made it sound as though I'd called the devil and reversed the charges.

"To check out Gryson," I said, wishing I'd left her lying on the gravel with Green Anorak rolling around on top of her. "And there's something weird about him, because the bloke on the other end hadn't heard of him. But when I gave him Miss Tibberton's address and told him there were burglars there, he started acting like it was all perfectly normal and he knew all about it. It just doesn't make sense."

"So you thought you'd come and tell us all about it?"

"I was only trying to help. Not you," I added nastily, "Miss Tibberton."

That shut her up for a moment. I was really seething. She chucked away the daisy and picked a piece of grass, which she started chewing. The hair masked her face, so all I could see was the tip of her nose. She couldn't even bear to look at me. I didn't know what she was thinking about me but I could guess. I got angrier and angrier. The silence got longer. I wanted her to say something so I could snap back at her. She wouldn't even give me that satisfaction.

"Well, what would you have done?" I demanded at last. "Imagine it: someone smashes up the flat of a friend of yours and shoots her cat." Miss Tibberton wasn't exactly a friend of mine but Smith wasn't to know that. "Then she runs off with someone she *says* is her niece. And that" – here I got slightly sarcastic – "is a little bit odd because she once told me she hadn't any relations. Then another lot of people walk into her flat. They say they're cops but they beat you up and generally act as if robbery with violence is more their line of business. Strikes you as normal, does it? The sort of thing that happens every day in a big city?" I snorted. Actually I was almost enjoying myself. "Well, maybe that's the way you do things in the States but it's not the way we do it here."

I paused but she still didn't say anything. She stared at the ground and chewed that piece of grass. Suddenly I wasn't angry any more – just scared. Whatever it was, this thing was too big for me. And too dangerous. I know my limitations and I'd been rubbing up against them for the last hour. It wasn't comfortable.

"You know what we should do?"

Her shoulders twitched. I took it to mean that nothing I could suggest was likely to have the slightest value whatsoever.

"Walk into the nearest police station."

There was no reaction from Smith.

"There's someone out there with a gun," I went on. It was the first time either of us had brought the word into the open. "If Gryson really is a cop, they may not be very nice to us. But they're not going to shoot us. Anyway, it's quite likely he isn't."

It was the sensible thing to do – anyone could see that. It wasn't something I wanted to do. In our part of the world you grow up with the idea that the less you have to do with the police, the better. But we didn't really have a choice. It was time to swallow our prejudices, just like the headmaster is always telling us to do in Assembly.

I was still staring at Smith. She wasn't moving. She'd even stopped chewing the blade of grass. It was lying on the ground just below her face.

"Well? If you won't, I will."

A drop of water fell on to the blade of grass. Another one landed beside it. Smith's shoulders twitched again. I could see her shoulder blades moving under the sweatshirt.

Oh God, I thought. She's crying. I felt at least three things: embarrassed, because someone crying is embarrassing; guilty, because I'd made her cry; and annoyed, because crying wasn't going to get either of us out of the mess we were in.

She turned her head so I could see her face. There were tear tracks through the grime on both cheeks. I'd never made a girl cry before, not since infants' school and that doesn't count. It made me feel awful.

"Not the police," she said. "Please, Chris."

That was another first – the first time she'd actually used my name.

"Why not?" I spoke gruffly, but then I had to go and spoil the effect by finding a paper handkerchief in my pocket and giving it to her.

She blew her nose. "I just can't go to the cops. Okay?"

"You'll have to tell me more."

"I can't."

"Why not?"

Smith looked at me for a moment. It was as if she were trying to memorize my face. Then she sighed and said, "Okay, but only if you promise not to go to the cops."

It was an unreasonable condition and I should have told her to go to hell. Instead I nodded.

"My dad's in trouble. Miss Tibberton was . . . helping us." She spoke slowly, choosing her words with care. "He's done nothing wrong, I swear it. Nothing illegal."

"But the police think he has?"

"Sort of."

It wasn't much of an answer but it was the only one she would give me. I tried another line: "So why did you come here?"

"Because it wasn't safe at Miss Tibberton's apartment. You saw the mess it was in. Someone turned the place over while she was out."

"And killed Pseud."

"I guess so." She shivered.

"Why?"

"They were looking for something. And killing the cat was maybe a warning for her." She screwed up her face and for a moment I thought she was going to start crying again.

"What were they looking for?" I said quickly.

"Something that could help Dad."

"Where did you stay last night?"

Apparently this part of the story wasn't top secret. Smith got quite talkative. Long before this business blew up, Miss Tibberton had rented a self-catering flatlet for a fortnight's holiday. She was going to spend her time doing what she liked best: taking pictures of big cats. The point was, it made a perfect bolthole because no one knew about it. Another reason to come here was to fetch something that could help Smith's father. She wouldn't tell me what it was.

"Let me get this straight," I said. "Miss Tibberton hid whatever it was here, and you two came to get it. So who's got it now?"

"No one. We were just going to get it when . . ."

Her voice tailed away. She hadn't told me what happened when Miss Tibberton was shot and in a way I was glad. It had all happened so fast that maybe Smith had seen no more than me.

"It's hidden in the zoo," I said. It was not a question; more like an inspiration.

"How did you know that?" Her face was hard and suspicious.

"The same way I knew you'd be here. I overheard her saying something about big cats and going fishing. Then she sort of laughed."

"She's kind of weird, isn't she?" Smith said unexpectedly. For once we were in total agreement. "I know it's at the zoo, but I don't know where."

"We could go and look." I added hastily: "Not now, of course."

"But where?"

"We could try asking her."

"You crazy?"

The answer was probably yes, but I went on: "Someone shot her, right? So she'll be in hospital." There was another possibility I didn't mention: that she was in a mortuary. "If we find out where, we may be able to see her."

I didn't believe that for a moment. If she was in hospital, the Bill would be very interested in anyone who wanted to visit her. I was just trying to cheer Smith up by assuming that Miss Tibberton was still alive. Stupid, really.

"She'll need her pills," Smith said suddenly.

"What're you talking about?"

"I don't know what they're for but she has to have them. She said so last night. That's why we were late going to the zoo. We had to find a pharmacy that was open and get some more. I've got them here." She produced a bottle of pills from the pocket of her jeans.

"Why've *you* got them?" I asked.

"Because she gave them to me to carry when we came out of the shop; I never had a chance to give them back to her." Smith studied the label while I studied her. "I can't read it."

"Here. Let me try." I couldn't read it either. The words on the label were just a scrawl in blue Biro. "Maybe she's diabetic."

"Or epileptic."

"Or she's got leukaemia."

"Or something." Smith sniffed. "Oh God, I wish we *knew*."

I don't think she meant the name of Miss Tibberton's illness. She was talking about the possibility I hadn't mentioned.

"We can find out," I said rashly. "They'll have taken her to hospital." *Or the mortuary*. "I'll find a phone box and ask. I'll say I'm a relative."

"Will you?" She gave me a smile whose existence I hadn't even suspected till now.

"And if she's there," I went on airily, "we'll find some way to get the pills to her. Leave it to me."

In the event it was just as well she didn't.

CHAPTER NINE

We prowled round the streets for nearly an hour. It was hard to concentrate because almost anyone we met could be a plain-clothes policeman. Anyway, most of the telephone boxes had been vandalized. In the end we found one that worked outside a row of little shops in a side road.

I dialled Directory Enquiries, explained that a friend of mine had been in an accident today and asked for the phone number of the nearest Casualty Department.

Smith offered to do the phoning but I pointed out they'd notice an American accent. She said she hadn't much accent left, because she'd been living in England for nearly eighteen months. I told her that if she sounded English then I sounded like the Prince of Wales. We had another argument about it. Then I phoned the Infirmary.

A woman answered. I'd been expecting to have a long delay while she hunted through the record of admissions, even to have to try another hospital. And that was assuming that Miss Tibberton *was* in a hospital. But as soon as I mentioned her name the receptionist said she'd switch me through to the ward. She sounded flustered. I heard the phone ring once on an extension, and then a man's voice came through.

"Ward 14. Can I help you?"

"You've got a Miss Tibberton in there?"

"That's correct," he said. "Who's calling?"

"Her nephew. Is she very ill?"

"Critical," the man said, which wasn't very informative. "But she's conscious. What name — ?"

"Can I speak to her?"

"Not just at present. The doctor's with her. But if you

leave your name and number, she should be able to call you back in about ten minutes."

"That's okay," I said. "I'll ring her."

I put the phone down and told Smith what the bloke had said.

"Thank God," she said. "I thought maybe . . ."

"Me too." I hesitated. "But the set-up stinks."

"How d'you mean?"

I shrugged. "It was all so efficient, somehow. When my gran was dying in hospital it wasn't like that." I remembered telephones that went on ringing for ever and staff who never quite seemed certain which patient was which. "And the man wanted to know my name and where I was. Why didn't he just ask me to call back later?"

"You figure it's a trap?" She nodded slowly, answering the question herself. "They were trying to put a trace on us."

"Those pills," I said.

Smith looked grimly at me. "We'll have to take them to her."

"We?" It seemed to me that she was taking a lot for granted. She just looked at me and I felt myself going red. "Yeah, all right."

We made a plan, or rather Smith made a plan and I said "Okay" at intervals. The first thing we did was go into one of the shops. It was one of those mini-markets run by Asians that sell almost everything. We got a packet of envelopes – they didn't sell them singly – a notepad and a Biro. I said I was starving so we also got four cans of Coke, some crisps and a packet of biscuits. Smith paid for everything with a five-pound note. I asked the bloke behind the counter how to get to the Infirmary. I was sure he was memorizing our features as he told us.

We trailed back to the garden in the square. It was beginning to feel like home. I started eating while Smith wrote a letter. When she'd finished, she handed it to me to read. I said her handwriting was illegible, which was true because it looked like a regiment of spiders bending to the right before a strong west wind. She scowled at me but wrote it out again in block capitals. This is what she said:

To Whom It May Concern:
Miss Tibberton, Ward 14, urgently needs these tablets.
You will have to find out what they are for. I don't know.

She put the pills and the letter in one of the envelopes, sealed it up and wrote Miss Tibberton's name and ward number on the outside.

"What about fingerprints?" I said.

"It doesn't matter for me," she said. She wouldn't explain why but I guessed she meant that the police already knew who she was.

We walked down the hill to the Infirmary. It was an old building that had sprouted modern wings in unexpected places. When we got there, we didn't go inside – it would have been too risky. If it really was a trap, we'd be walking into an ambush.

Smith's plan was simple. We'd go to the visitors' car park and ask someone who was visiting to hand in the package at Reception on their way in.

It was a good plan but it didn't work out. The car park was full but, when we arrived, there was no one there. So we hung around for a few minutes, feeling paranoid. A lot of windows overlooked the car park and anyone could be watching us.

Smith nudged my arm. A VW Scirocco GTi nosed into the car park. A nice motor – a few years old, but it looked brand new. It drove slowly along the lines of parked cars, searching for a space.

"It's a woman," Smith said. "She'll do."

The Scirocco reversed neatly into a slot at the end

of the row where we were standing. A tall, fair-haired woman got out. She was maybe thirty yards away and she was alone.

"You stay here," Smith said. She started walking.

The woman turned as she locked the door and I saw her profile. She reminded me of something that belonged in a stable.

The recognition jolted me like an elbow in the stomach. I knew *what* she was, if not *who* she was. I leapt forward and grabbed Smith's arm. She squawked. I pulled her into the gap between a Transit van and a Ford Escort and told her to shut up.

The woman's heels clicked towards us on the tarmac. I realized she was actually going to pass us on her way to the main entrance. I dragged Smith down the side of the van. There was just room to squeeze between the back of it and the wall behind.

The rhythm of the heels slowed and I nearly stopped breathing. Then it picked up again. Gradually the sound grew less as she moved away.

Smith hissed in my ear: "Do you think you could possibly stop *mauling* me?"

I let go of her arm as quickly as if it had suddenly turned into one of those electric cattle prods. As far as this girl was concerned, anything I did seemed to be wrong.

"Sorry," I mumbled.

"I sure as hell hope you've got an explanation," she said in the sort of voice you use on Barry Sinclair when he's done something particularly gross.

"That woman," I snapped back (as far as you can snap in a whisper), "she's the one I saw last night at the flat. Gryson's boss. The one he called 'madam'."

"You sure?"

I just looked at her.

She gave a little sigh. "Okay, I guess I overreacted." That was all the apology I was going to get. She looked away from me and changed the subject. "It's not that surprising, I guess. You'd expect to find her here."

"The vultures gather?"

"Uh huh. We'll have to find someone else."

The next people to reach the car park came on foot from the hospital, so they were no use to us. They were two men, one in his twenties and the other maybe fifteen years older. Smith and I scuttled back behind the Transit. I didn't know about her but I was getting more and more nervous. I'd have been ready to suspect a toddler of being a fully paid-up police informant.

The men paused in front of the Metro that was parked on the other side of the Escort. I guessed they knew each other but had come in separate cars.

The older one lit a cigarette. "That was a waste of time."

"There's a story there, Jack," the other said. "The place was crawling with Special Branch."

"Yeah, but we can't use it. They'll slap a D Notice on it if we tried. Especially nowadays."

"You think it's the same woman?"

"Of course it bloody is. It's not exactly a common surname."

"A shooting incident near the funfair. A middle-aged woman involved. Rushed to the Infirmary but dead on arrival. Bank Holiday mystery killing, you know the sort of line. They can't object to that, can they?"

"Just try it," Jack said, jingling his car keys. "They'll drop the Official Secrets Act on you from a great height. And when you finally crawl out from underneath, you'd better start thinking of a change of career. No editor's going to employ you."

"Ah, come off it."

"I'm serious, lad. If you don't believe me, try it and see."

Jack got into the Metro and drove away. The other bloke walked past us to a rusty Renault near the Scirocco. After a moment he drove away, too.

Neither of us wanted to say anything. I don't know about Smith but I was streaming with sweat – it was oozing out of every pore.

Smith cleared her throat. "Dead on arrival," she said in a small, tight voice. "So it was a trap."

All I could think of was Miss Tibberton looking down at a print I'd done a few weeks ago in her darkroom. It was a shot of a battered old angel in the Kensal Green cemetery. I'd had to lie on the grave to get the angle right. All she'd said was, "I've seen worse, Chris". Then there had been a pause before she went on to tell me how I could have done it better.

"The bastards," I said softly.

I don't know if Smith heard me. "Special Branch?" she said. "What's that?"

"They're police." I remembered a documentary I'd seen on TV. "They do a lot of work for MI5, the security service. All the arresting and stuff like that." I'd spoken automatically and it took a few seconds for what I'd said to sink into my mind. I spun round and stared at her. "What the hell is this?"

Now I was even more scared than I'd been before. The more I got involved in this business the worse it became. I felt as though I'd been sucked into a whirlpool: I was going round, faster and faster, in ever-decreasing circles, and pretty soon I'd drown.

"Chris," Smith said. "You got to trust me. *Please*."

"That's what I've been doing," I said bitterly. "And look where it's got me."

"I'm sorry — "

"That's not good enough," I yelled. "It's about time you told me what's going on. Either that or I'm going."

It sounded tough but I didn't feel that way inside. I had an awful suspicion that I was in too far to get out. I mean, you can't just paddle out of a whirlpool. Gryson and Green Anorak knew I'd gone to find Miss Tibberton; they knew I'd helped Smith. By now they were after me as well, and Green Anorak had a personal reason to get even with me. It was so damned unfair.

"I can't explain right now," Smith said. "But I will, I promise."

"It's too late," I said.

I'd had enough. I walked away from her without a backward glance, though I won't pretend I wasn't listening to hear if she followed. I went down the line of parked cars towards the entrance.

A red Sierra drove in. The three digits on the number plate were the same as the last ones of our phone number – 941. The window was down and the driver glanced incuriously at me. He had a grey face and grey bristly hair. I knew I'd seen him before recently.

I walked on. I just didn't want to know. About anything. Smith's footsteps were behind me. I think she was almost running.

There was a screech as the car braked.

"So there you are," a man's voice said. He could only have been talking to Smith: there was no one else to talk to. "I've been looking for you all over. I've a message from your father."

CHAPTER TEN

"Who are you?" Smith said. She sounded short of breath. Or terrified.

I stopped and glanced back. In that split-second I knew where I'd seen the man before. A long face with grey, bristly hair that stood up like a brush. This time he wasn't wearing a navy-blue raincoat and the length of the legs and arms wasn't obvious because he was sitting in the car.

But all the same I was certain. It was the humanoid spider who'd nearly barged into me in Endymion Street yesterday. Just before I found Pseud's body.

"My name doesn't matter," the man said. They were so wrapped up in each other that neither of them noticed me walking back towards them. "Your father's got away. He wants you to join him."

When I heard him speak before, he'd been snarling at me. Right now he was almost cooing. There was something about the way he said "father" and "wants" that made me wonder if English wasn't his first language.

"Where is he?" Smith said.

"Quite near. Hop in, and I'll take you."

She touched the handle of the offside rear door.

It was too big a coincidence. Hanging around Miss Tibberton's flat and now visiting the hospital where she lay dead. He had to be one of Gryson's men.

"Wait a minute," I said.

They both glanced at me. Smith hesitated a moment too long. The man was out of the car and towering over her. He seized her arm and hauled her towards the car.

I grabbed her other arm. It was a tug of war, and I was losing.

Then the miracle happened. The humanoid spider let go. Smith and I nearly fell over. He leapt into the car, gunned the engine and shot off round the car park to the exit on the far side. Seconds later, the Sierra was gone.

"Hey, you!"

It was the tall woman, Gryson's boss. She was sprinting towards us as fast as her high heels would let her.

Somewhere in my mind the penny dropped. If the humanoid spider was running away, that could only mean—

But there was no time for reflection. Smith and I were running too. If this goes on, I remember thinking, I won't have to train for the next marathon.

The woman didn't have a chance, which made a nice change for us. The high heels were too much of a handicap. By the time we'd followed the Sierra through the exit and on to the main road, we'd nearly doubled our lead. On the left was a bus stop and a double-decker was just pulling away. It was the old-fashioned sort with an open platform at the back.

I leapt on. There was a thud and a gasp as Smith followed. She only just managed to grab the pole.

"That could have been nasty," the conductor said.

"Yeah," I said. "It could."

I asked for tickets to the end of the line but we left the bus at the next stop. A whole crowd of people got off there, and I don't think the conductor noticed us leaving. We zigzagged away from the main road and ended up in the little park in the middle of our square. There was nowhere else to go. This time it felt even more like home.

Neither of us spoke till we'd had a drink and found a patch of grass that was in the shade.

"That bloke," I said. "You know him?"

Smith shook her head. She'd been pale ever since I'd met her, but now she seemed even paler.

I told her where and when I'd seen him. "I thought he was Special Branch, at first. But he ran away when he saw that woman. He's got to belong to the opposition."

"The guys who wrecked Miss Tibberton's apartment?"

"And killed Pseud."

"Not just that," she said in a sour voice. "There's a whole lot more."

I waited for her to go on, but it was another one of her enigmatic remarks that she wasn't inclined to explain to the likes of me.

After a while I said, "I'm going back to London."

"You're crazy," Smith said. She didn't sound angry, just hopeless. "They know who you are and where you live. They'll catch up with you. Either Gryson or the guy in the red car."

"I can stay with a friend."

"For ever?"

"But I haven't done anything," I said.

"Oh yeah? You've helped me, haven't you? You heard what those reporters were saying." She mimicked a British accent: "It's not cricket, is it?" Her voice went back to normal: "You might as well face it: this is a different ball game and there aren't any rules. If there's a referee someone will have shot him by now. Like they shot Miss Tibberton. You think they'll leave you on the loose? Don't be stupid. You know too much."

"I don't know *anything*."

I was thinking of my whirlpool. The only way left was to take a deep breath and let the current drag me down. And hope that whirlpools had got a worse reputation than they deserved.

Okay, Smith was right: I couldn't pretend that nothing had happened.

"What are you going to do?" I asked.

"I figured on going to the zoo."

"You're mad."

She shook her head. "They don't know that Miss Tibberton hid something there. It's the last place they'll expect me to go because it's so close to where she was shot. Anyway, I've run out of options."

The vital piece of evidence, I thought – the whatever-it-was she had to find to save her father from whatever trouble he was in. That's what was driving her.

I remembered another bit of the conversation I'd overheard while she and Miss Tibberton were getting into their taxi. It was less than twenty-four hours ago but it felt like years.

"Talking of options," I said casually, "what about Kellaway? Are you going to him after you've been to the zoo?"

Smith did a double-take, then realized how I knew the name. "What's it got to do with you?"

"It might have quite a lot."

"You're coming with me?" She sounded as if she didn't believe me.

I shrugged. I wasn't sure I believed myself. "You're not the only one who's run out of options."

There were two entrances to the zoo. We chose the one that wasn't opposite the funfair. I bought the ticket and we filed through the turnstile.

It was mid-afternoon. The sky was blue and the place was packed. I hate zoos – all those miserable animals looking dignified in their cages while the human animals giggle at them. I don't know why but most people start behaving like mentally-retarded baboons when they visit a zoo. I can understand why Miss Tibberton preferred cats to people.

The site was shaped like a square with a corner bitten out of it by a large mammal. It was laid out like a garden, with lots of grass, trees, winding paths, ornamental pools and flowerbeds. In the middle was an old house that had been turned into offices, a cafeteria and exhibition rooms.

"It could be *anywhere*," Smith said gloomily.

"It might help if you told me what we're looking for."

"She didn't say. You know what she was like."

"Then what did she say?"

Smith bit her lip. "That she'd hidden something here that would save my father. She'd put it here because the flat wasn't safe. She said it was somewhere in public where no one would think of looking."

That was a great help. For the next half-hour we trailed round the zoo. Both of us kept looking over our shoulders, which made it hard to concentrate. We both knew it was unlikely that anyone would look for us here: but knowing is one thing, believing another.

The jabbering of the other visitors began to get on my nerves. The animals were okay – most of them just ignored us. The things I remember are the stench of the polar bears and an enormous, mud-brown elephant that just stood in its dusty enclosure, doing absolutely nothing.

"This is pointless," Smith said at last.

I'd been thinking the same thing but hadn't liked to mention it. We were standing beside the aviary. A few yards away a parrot cackled, as though it were mocking our failure. The cackle was uncannily like Miss Tibberton's laugh. She didn't laugh very often. I suddenly recalled the last time I'd heard her.

"Do you remember yesterday?" I said. "When she was talking about coming down here? She said something about going fishing."

Smith shrugged. "She probably didn't mean anything. Just that we were going to look for something."

"But she might have meant it literally. Come on, it's worth a try."

I dragged us round all the places where fish were. Not just the aquarium. The penguins and the polar bears were fed with fish. It wasn't much of an idea but at the time it seemed better than nothing.

Most of the live fish were behind glass. All the dead fish we could see were in the process of being gobbled up. We drifted back towards the big cats. Smith slumped down on a low wall that surrounded one of the ornamental ponds.

"I give up," she said in a low, unsteady voice.

"We've only just begun," I said brightly. As she went down, I went up. Anyway, I didn't want her to start crying again. "Maybe we should try and see it through her eyes. If you were her and wanted to hide something here, where would you put it?"

I sat down beside her. She was staring at the lilies that covered most of the pond.

"Well?" I realized she wasn't going to answer, so I plodded on. "It'd have to be somewhere she could get to, which rules out all the cages and offices and things. It'd have to be — "

"Chris," she said. "Did you see that?"

"What?"

She pointed at a spot in the middle of the pond that was clear of lilies. Something moved beneath the surface – a flash of orange.

"Goldfish," she said. "And this is the nearest pond to the big cats. What did she say? *We're going fishing.*"

I rolled up my sleeve and pushed my arm into the water. I couldn't touch the bottom. So the pond was at least two feet deep.

"She wouldn't just chuck something in," Smith went on. "Not if she wanted to find it again."

"And she wouldn't put it in the middle," I said, "because everyone would notice when she tried to get it out."

Smith tugged up the sleeves of her sweatshirt. There was a bruise on one of her arms, either from Green Anorak or from the man in the Sierra.

"You go that way," she said, "and I'll go this way, and we'll meet on the other side and work our way back again. Then we'll try the other ponds."

"Okay, boss," I said meekly.

We plunged our hands into the water and explored the stems on the lilies and the slimy masonry of the retaining wall. The lilies themselves were planted in submerged plastic baskets that rested on brick columns. Once a fish brushed against my hand and I let out a yelp of surprise. Several passers-by looked curiously at us but no one interfered. We took a break while someone in a uniform sauntered past – the average zoo official would probably think that we were trying to poach their precious goldfish.

A moment later, Smith stood up and turned away from the pool. I thought she'd seen someone coming, so I stopped too. Then she grinned at me and stuffed something in the pocket of her jeans.

I started laughing, God knows why. And she laughed back at me and for a moment she seemed a different person.

"Tea," Smith said. "Yuk."

"There's nothing wrong with tea."

I set down the tray on the table. We were in the cafeteria at the zoo. I'd bought just a Coke for her because she said she wasn't hungry.

"Tannin?" she said challengingly. "Caffeine? Your metabolism's a disaster area." Little Miss Know-All's eyes swivelled between the cheese sandwich and the Mars Bar that flanked my cup of tea. "Do you never stop eating?"

I remembered something I'd heard in a history lesson. "According to Napoleon, an army marches on its stomach."

"So do worms."

It wasn't meant as a joke. We'd stopped laughing some time ago. We were back to normal. She'd refused to tell me what she'd found in the pond. Instead she'd gone off to examine it in the privacy of the ladies' lavatory. It's nice to feel trusted.

"What's bugging you now?" I said.

I reckoned it was safe to talk. At the next table a man and a woman were having a quarrel in hushed, hissing voices that occasionally soared in volume when they got really narked with each other. They certainly weren't listening to us, and there was no one else within earshot.

"I'm sorry," Smith said unexpectedly. "I guess I shouldn't take it out on you."

"What's the problem?" I spoke through a mouthful of cheese sandwich. "You've got what you wanted, haven't you?"

"It was a little polythene bag," she said quietly, deciding to trust me with a crumb of information. "Weighted with a stone and wedged in a crack between two of the bricks. And inside was another bag, sealed with a knot. And then another and another."

"Chinese boxes," I said.

She ignored me. "And right inside was a little canister with Scotch tape round the lid. And inside that was a negative."

"You're being irrational," the man at the next table said. "Just like a woman."

"Irrational?" the woman said, equally loudly. "Just listen to yourself. You're about as rational as one of those monkeys over there. What about the time when . . ."

Their voices dropped back to the old level.

"Black-and-white?" I asked automatically. "Or colour?"

"Black-and-white," Smith said miserably.

I wasn't surprised to hear that it was a negative. The canister sounded like one of those containers for 35mm film. After all, Miss Tibberton had been a photographer. What did surprise me was Smith's reaction. I thought she'd be over the moon.

"I held it up to the light," she went on, "but I couldn't see anything except lots of people. Some sort of crowd scene, maybe."

"What were you hoping for?"

"I don't know. Something that made sense. Something that'd clear my father."

"Miss Tibberton must have had a reason for putting it here," I said. "You need to get it printed."

"Would that be easy?"

"Sure. There're lots of places that do a same-day service." I saw her face light up. "But you'll have to wait till Tuesday. Everywhere'll be closed tomorrow." The light went out in her face. "I could do it myself if I could get to a darkroom."

I just wanted to cheer her up. In fact I wasn't sure if I could do the printing: I knew the theory but I hadn't had much practice.

"You know what your trouble is?" As the woman at the next table got angrier, her voice steadily rose in volume. "Sexism! Old-fashioned, common-or-garden sexism."

"Don't be *ridiculous*," the man said coldly.

Both Smith and I glanced at them. Even when you're smothered by your own problems, the temptation to eavesdrop on other people's quarrels is irresistible.

The woman was about six foot four and wore a brown dress like a sack. She waved a teaspoon at the bloke. "You think you're a liberated male just because you go to the laundrette once in a while. Oh yes, and don't let's forget that you know how to cook frozen peas. Liberated *crap!* You're a male chauvinist pig, just like your father."

Her companion went pink and spluttered at her. Smith tore herself away. I suppose we didn't have time for spectator sports.

"Have you got a darkroom?" she asked. "Or access to one?"

I shook my head, feeling relieved that my skills weren't going to be put to the test.

"I know Kellaway has."

That was the third time Kellaway's name had come up.

"Can you use it?" I said.

"I'm not sure." She glanced at me over her glass. For once she decided to give me a straight answer. "He's a friend of Dad's. But I don't know if I can trust him. I don't know if I can trust anyone."

I decided not to take it personally. "What are you going to do?"

"I don't know."

"Feminism," the man said, "shouldn't be mutually exclusive of femininity."

"Are you implying I'm unfeminine?" the woman snarled. "And stop being so pompous."

"You'll need to find somewhere to sleep," I said. So did I. "How are you off for money?"

"That's not a problem." She said that casually, as if money had never been a problem in her entire life. "But I can't just walk into somewhere and ask for a room. They'll warn all the hotels and places. I'll have to find a park bench or someplace like that."

"We'd be safer in London."

"How come?"

"For a start, they're looking for us here. And this isn't a big city. We don't even know it well. Where do you live?"

"London," Smith said absently. "When I'm not at school or in the States."

Boarding school? I might have known. That's where the airs and graces came from.

"But I can't go home," she went on. "They'll be watching our apartment. They nearly caught me there on Saturday morning."

"Still, at least we know where we are in London." I wondered if Barry's mum would put us both up; I know she's easy-going but there might be limits to her tolerance. Also, she's dead nosy.

Smith thought of another objection: "How do we get there? They'll be watching the roads and the trains and the buses."

It was a depressing thought. Special Branch could arrange almost anything. A nationwide alert for two teenagers was peanuts as far as they were concerned.

"That does it!" the woman at the next table yelled. "That really does it! And I'll tell you another thing: you can find your own way home."

The man pushed back his chair and stood up. He had short, stumpy legs and the sort of hair that's meant to go with hot tempers. "Well, thank God for that," he bellowed. "I've never met such a bloody awful driver."

She snorted. "What you mean," she said patronizingly, "is that I don't treat my car like an offensive weapon in the middle of a battlefield. If they banned male drivers, there'd be no more accidents."

"Frankly," the boyfriend said, "I'd rather go by train." He picked up his jacket, which was hanging on the back of his chair. "At least I'll get there in the end."

"I'm quite capable of — "

"It's not just a question of your capacity as a driver," the bloke interrupted with a nasty grin, "doubtful though that is. There's also the small matter of the capacity of your fuel tank. Plus the fact that accidentally on purpose you left your money at home. Being mean never pays. Poetic justice, you might say."

"What are you talking about?"

"The needle of your fuel gauge is on the red, my dear." He really was enjoying himself; you could practically see the pleasure oozing out of him. "If you're lucky, you might have thirty miles left in the tank. But there'll almost certainly be traffic jams, and they aren't good for fuel consumption."

"You little toad," the woman said.

"No cash," the man said happily, "no cheque book, no credit cards. You wouldn't even join the AA because you said it cost too much. I really don't know what you're going to do."

He gave her a toad-like smile and sauntered out of the cafeteria. To do her justice, the woman didn't try to call him back. She shut her mouth very tightly and stared into her empty teacup.

I looked at Smith and she looked at me. Then I got up and went over to the woman.

"Excuse me — "

"Yes?" she barked at me. "What is it?"

"We couldn't help hearing. Are you going back to London?"

84

I thought she'd bite my head off but instead she just nodded wearily.

"Me and my friend need a lift. We'd pay."

It was not a comfortable journey for a lot of reasons.

First off, the Toad was quite right: the woman, who introduced herself as Gemma, really was a bloody awful driver. Secondly, she drove a clapped-out Mini with a hole in its silencer and a habit of stalling when the engine idled. Thirdly, the motorway was mostly traffic jam, which meant (among other things) that we did a lot of idling and the engine did a lot of stalling. Fourthly, Smith and I couldn't talk to one another, and Smith couldn't even open her mouth, except for the occasional grunt, because her accent was too much of a giveaway. Fifthly, it was horribly hot in that little car. And sixthly, Gemma never stopped moaning about the Toad.

You get the picture. Smith was lucky – she sat in the back so she didn't have to listen to Gemma's voice clacking away. As part of my job I had to say "Yes", "No" and "*Really*" at the right moments. This was easy enough in theory but in practice I kept dozing off for a few seconds or worrying about what we were going to do when we hit London. The only good point about it was that she was talking so much that she didn't turn on the radio. I was afraid that the police might put out a newsflash about us.

The one interesting thing that happened was right at the beginning, before we reached the motorway, when Smith gave me some money to pay for the petrol. When I saw the bundle of notes she pulled out of her pocket, I nearly fainted. She had a great big wodge of tens and twenties. Like she said, money wasn't a problem.

What with the traffic and the fact that the Mini's top speed was 55 m.p.h. downhill, the journey took twice as long as it had done in the coach this morning. This time I couldn't insulate myself with Paul Anders. Gemma might have thought I wasn't listening to her.

When we got to London, she let us out just before Hammersmith. She was going to Fulham and I said vaguely we were going somewhere else. We got out of the car. I bent down and said "Thanks" through the open window. Gemma said, "The bloody toad" one more time and drove off without indicating into the stream of traffic. I hope she got home. We started walking towards the tube station.

Smith said, "Now what?"

Good question. Both our homes were no-go areas. All my friends were away. All except Barry Sinclair, and the more I thought about him and his parents, the less I liked the idea of staying with them.

But I had one idea. The trouble was, I couldn't tell Smith because I knew she wouldn't like the way I'd have to present it. Anyway, it probably wouldn't work.

"Money's no object, right?" I said to her.

"Up to a point. Why?"

I shrugged. "It could be important."

We found a phone box. I had a handful of change in my pocket.

"Can you stay outside?" I said to Smith.

"Who are you calling?"

"It's kind of private. You keep watch."

We had another argument but in the end she stayed outside.

CHAPTER TWELVE

Barry Sinclair was waiting for us by the barrier at the station. The cat basket was by his feet, with the carrier bag I'd given him beside it. Oh God. I'd completely forgotten about Alias.

"Hi," Barry said, leering at Smith. "You got here okay? Great!"

He has this genius for stating the obvious.

I said, "This is Mary."

Smith forced a smile on her face and said, "Hi."

"Hi," he said again, examining her as carefully as he dared. He was still wearing the leather jacket, despite the heat, and he'd just combed his hair. He thought he was really something.

I guessed he was comparing Smith with Dawn Fisher and for some reason that made me angry.

"You got the key?" I said.

"Sure. Took a little work, but no problem." He sounded like a property tycoon who'd just closed a complicated deal on a skyscraper rather than someone who'd just rifled his father's office. "Of course there're still a few – uh – details we need to iron out."

He meant the money, of course. Thirty quid, in advance; Barry didn't believe in credit.

"When we get there," I said firmly.

He tore his eyes away from Smith. "One more thing." He gave the cat basket a nudge with his foot. "You have to take that animal with you. Otherwise the deal's off."

That was something Barry hadn't mentioned on the phone.

"Come off it," I said. "You'll have him for another day, won't you? Maybe we could— "

"It's not a question of money," Barry said, and I knew at once he was deadly serious. "I mean, that animal's feral. It's terrorized my kid sister. It belongs in a zoo, if you ask me. Look what it did." He pulled up his cuff and showed us two parallel scratches on his wrist. "My parents say it ought to be put down."

"He'll soon settle, once he's— "

"Sorry, Chris, but I'm really not prepared to negotiate on this point. I know two's company" – the leer was back on his face – "but he's not staying with me."

I glanced at Smith, hoping she hadn't added the leers to the "two's company" remark and come up with the answer that was in Barry's mind. She was looking at him with morbid fascination, as though he was the one that belonged in a zoo.

"We'll talk about it later," I said quickly. "Come on, we haven't got all day."

"In a hurry, are we?" Barry grinned and I wanted to hit him. "Where's your luggage, Mary?"

Smith just stared at him. It was interesting to see her putting down someone who wasn't me. It made a change. Barry wilted. He rubbed his chin, which he always does when he's nervous. And that was a mistake because one of his spots burst under the pressure. He was in such a state that he actually picked up the carrier bag, rather than left it to me to carry. The bag was even heavier than the basket because of the tins and the cat-litter.

The shop was at least half a mile from the station. The neighbourhood is what my mother calls "not very nice", which means it's even rougher than where we live. Imagine Endymion Street on a larger scale and you get the picture.

Barry soon recovered his confidence. He started lecturing Smith on the brilliant commercial openings that exist in depressed urban areas and dropping hints about the size of his father's turnover. He generally gave the impression that the only reason he'd come here by public transport was that his mum was using the second Rolls-Royce.

After all the build-up, the shop itself was a bit of a letdown. It was a tiny place, squeezed between a hamburger joint and a greengrocer's. The pavement was ankle-deep in empty cartons and cans. Judging by the window display, most of the stock consisted of dustbin liners and soap. Barry unlocked a door just beyond the shop.

We found ourselves in a covered alleyway between the drugstore and the greengrocer's. At the other end was a yard that both shops shared. The air smelled of fried food. There were big double gates at the back. I guessed the yard was used for deliveries.

Barry unlocked one of the two doors at the rear of the building.

"The other door's to the shop. The flat's quite separate, of course," he added in his best estate agent's manner, "so we don't have to worry about the burglar alarm."

Inside the door was a flight of uncarpeted stairs. Alias's basket scraped against the wall and a shower of plaster fell off.

"For such a central location," Barry said as he led us upstairs, "it's really amazingly private. You could be anywhere."

There was another door at the head of the stairs. He unlocked it, put a hand in to switch on the light and stood aside with a flourish, so Smith and I could go in first. We were on a small, windowless landing. Four more doors opened on to it. Barry opened the nearest one on the left.

The room beyond was overpoweringly stuffy. I put down Alias's basket on the carpet and a cloud of dust mushroomed up. The window overlooked the yard. The glass was so dirty you hardly needed curtains.

"This is the lounge-diner." Barry tugged at the window but it wouldn't open. "As you see, it's fully furnished. Even a TV." He patted the portable black-and-white set that stood on a table by the blocked-off fireplace. "Crockery and cutlery in here" – he pointed at a sideboard that someone had painted white a long time ago – "and the electricity meter's behind the settee. You'll need fifty-pence pieces, by the way. Oh, and be careful of the sideboard. It's probably an antique."

Beside me, Smith coughed. It was the sort of cough that starts out as a laugh.

He went back on the landing and opened the next door. We peered into a little cupboard, perhaps six feet by four. There were three dead flies on the floor. I brushed a spider's web off my face.

"The kitchen," Barry announced. "The extractor fan is brand new, and so is the electric water heater. You can use that as a kettle if you want. You'll find saucepans and so on in the cupboard." He nudged me in the ribs. "Assuming you have any time for cooking."

"Is there any food here?" I said hastily, hoping that Smith hadn't heard the last bit.

"No. But there's a shop just round the corner that sells more or less everything. Now, here's the toilet."

You could tell that by the smell. He went in, glanced in the bowl and quickly pulled the chain. Smith wrinkled her nose.

"And finally . . ." He pushed open the fourth door and stood back. "The room you've all been waiting for."

I could have done without the commentary. The bedroom overlooked the main road. There was a stained mattress on the double bed, and two blankets that had once been pink. A wardrobe with no door and a chest of drawers.

"A double bed," Barry said. His eyebrows were working in all directions at once. "Naturally."

"But where's the bathroom?" Smith said in an aston-ished voice. "And I don't mean the john."

Barry got a bit pink and started rubbing his chin again. "Well, there's the sink in the kitchen— "

"You mean there's nowhere I can take a shower?"

"Not exactly. My father's thinking of— "

Smith gave him another one of her looks and he dried up in mid-sentence.

"Thanks, Barry," I said. "See you."

"Uh. I think that's it." He handed me a bunch of keys and sidled towards the front door. "Like I said on the phone, it's just for the one night, okay? It might be better not to switch on the light in the bedroom. Someone might notice. And for God's sake don't break anything. I'll come round tomorrow afternoon."

He actually got to the door before he remembered.

"I nearly forgot. The rent. We agreed on thirty-five, didn't we?"

"Thirty," I said grimly. "Don't push your luck."

Barry would have argued if Smith hadn't been there. She gave him a ten and a twenty. I could see his brain whirring when he realized that she was the one who had the money. He held up both notes to the light.

"You wouldn't believe the number of forgeries that are in circulation. My dad says— "

"See you tomorrow." I held the door open for him.

Even then he hesitated in the doorway, his eyes flicking from Smith to me. The trouble with Barry, you can't push him down for very long: he just bounces back.

"Have fun," he said with a knowing chuckle that didn't quite conceal the fact that he was as envious as hell. "Don't do anything I wouldn't do."

Smith waited until the door at the bottom of the stairs closed behind him. Then she turned on me. I took a step backwards.

"What did you say to that guy?"

"I told him we needed a place to stay."

"And?"

"Well, I couldn't tell him the truth, could I?"

"I get it. How dumb can you get? You had the nerve to make out that— "

"Can you think of a better idea?" I yelled. "It had to be something he'd believe."

"Are all your friends like that?" She was yelling, too. "Zit-covered zombies who can't think of anything except . . . Why are you laughing?"

It was the zit-covered zombie that creased me. Zits is a much better word than spots. It sounded right for Barry. They belonged together.

"The Big Zit," I spluttered.

Then Smith started laughing, too. It wasn't very funny. I suppose we'd reached the point where laughing was the only thing to do, and it didn't much matter what we laughed at.

We both stopped at the same time. I felt embarrassed and I think Smith did as well. She went into the living room and I followed. Alias yowled plaintively through the bars, reminding me that I was hungry.

"I'll take the bed," Smith said. "You can sleep there" – she nodded at the sofa, which was about four feet long and covered with shiny silver plastic – "with the cat. What about food?"

For the next half-hour, we were busy being domestic. It was like kids playing house. First we gave Alias his supper, after which he went to sleep on a chair. Smith found some rags and a dustpan and brush under the sink. If it'd been me, I wouldn't have touched any of the dirt but she had different ideas. Fifteen minutes' work made the bed, the sofa and the kitchen slightly less sordid than they had been. We left everything else.

Smith borrowed my towel and a clean T-shirt and had a wash in the sink while I went shopping. The T-shirt was my Paul Anders one, and she said "Yuk" when she saw it. She knew the name but she hadn't heard any of the music. I told her that most people I knew found it too sophisticated for them.

By now it was the middle of the evening but the shop round the corner was still open and doing a roaring trade. I bought lavatory paper, a toothbrush for Smith, milk, peanut butter, apples, yoghurt and sliced bread. Then I got us jumbo-size cheeseburgers, chips and coffee from the place next to the drugstore. Smith moaned about junk food but we both wanted something hot and there was no way either of us was going to do any cooking.

It was a weird meal. There we were, facing each other across the table, saying things like "Pass the salt" and "Do you want another bit of bread?" Smith had washed her hair while I was out and wrapped it in the towel. It was like we'd been living together for years. Only it wasn't like that at all because we hardly knew each other.

Maybe that was why we started asking one another questions. Nothing controversial, of course – just harmless stuff like where I lived and whether we had any brothers and sisters. I suppose we were trying to make things seem more normal by filling in the gaps.

I learned that her parents had divorced years ago when she was a kid, and that she'd always lived with her dad because her mum didn't want to be bothered with children. No brothers or sisters – just her father. He was a big shot in a multi-national, and they'd lent him to their British subsidiary for a three-year contract. The company paid her fees at boarding school. It was a big place on the south coast where they played lacrosse and were expected to behave like young ladies. Smith said it bore no relation to the real world, and also it was dreary. I said that my school was nothing but the real world and that was dreary too.

"Why Smith?" I asked at one point. "You must have a first name. Everyone does."

"Yeah – it's Polish. It was Mom's grandmother's name. I can't even pronounce it."

"What is it?"

Smith, who was piling peanut butter, slices of apple and yoghurt on to a piece of bread, shook her head. "That's one question I never answer."

"I thought there were quite a lot of questions like that."

There was a moment's silence and then she started asking about my family. It's funny but it seemed to fascinate her – she wanted every detail I could dredge up about Judith and Clive, for instance, and she also wanted to hear about my parents and their second honeymoon in Spain.

"It must be kind of strange," she said. "Having parents who actually do things together."

I shrugged. My parents are romantics, which is ridiculous at their age. To change the subject, I said, "Your father never married someone else?"

"No way. He just has girlfriends. Every year or so he trades in the old one for a new model."

We cleared away the meal as best we could – there was nowhere to put the rubbish and the water-heater wasn't working.

I tried to make her talk about tomorrow. For a start we needed a place to stay. How about Kellaway? I wanted to know.

"Can we leave it till morning?" she said. And she asked the question in such a hopeless way that I had to say okay. She started doing her teeth so I wandered back into the living room and turned on the TV. To my surprise it worked.

Some stupid gameshow was coming to an end. A young couple was getting hysterical about the fridge-freezer they'd just won. Then came the news.

As the theme music boomed out, it all flooded back into my mind – everything that had happened in the last thirty hours; everything we'd so carefully avoided talking about tonight. I nearly turned off the set.

But they'd already started reading the headlines: "An

American has been charged in connection with the Verdoli spy scandal . . . Police confirmed that there may be a link between Verdoli and the shooting today of a photographer formerly employed by the security services . . . The Bank-Holiday death toll on the roads has already reached double figures . . . Thousands of travellers have been stranded at Gatwick Airport . . . And in the United States the former White House Chief of Staff denies that— "

There was a sound behind me. I turned. Smith was standing in the doorway. Her face was grey but she was still holding the toothbrush.

"Drew Smith," the news reader droned on, "the American Deputy Director of Verdoli's Research and Development Department in the UK, has been charged with . . ."

"I guess you had to know sometime." Smith came into the room and sat down in front of the television.

I said nothing. I stared at Alias who was still asleep. He wasn't feral. Just a fat slob with a taste for the easy life. Who could blame him? I didn't.

"I was going to tell you tomorrow," she said in an urgent whisper. "I promise."

CHAPTER THIRTEEN

Now I know what a frozen silence is.

I thought it was one of those stupid phrases they use in books – the sort that don't really mean anything. In fact it means exactly what it says.

You're silent, obviously, because you don't say anything. You can't. The temperature seems to drop. It was hot in that room but I wanted to shiver. And you're frozen in another sense: you can't move. I stood by the sofa, hunched forward and totally still. My eyes were trained on that black-and-white screen. I couldn't even swivel my eyeballs a few degrees and look at Smith. Not wouldn't – couldn't.

In the frozen silence we watched and listened. Eventually – it seemed like years but can't have been more than a minute or two – the news reader started rabbitting on about normal things like motorway madness and holiday car crashes that shouldn't have happened. Normal things like death and disaster. You know something? They're only normal when they happen to someone else.

Smith got up and turned off the set.

"I guess I should have told you before," she said. "I knew you'd hear sooner or later." She sat down at one end of the sofa. "The first thing you've got to understand is that they've got the wrong guy."

I shrugged and left the room.

"Where you going? Chris, please listen."

Her control had snapped and she was on the verge of panic. Good. I went into the kitchen and filled myself a mug of water. I drank it slowly. She'd be waiting for the slam of the front door, for the sound of my feet on the stairs. It was a sort of revenge but it didn't taste sweet. I refilled the mug and went back to the living room. I guessed she would have liked me to sit on the sofa. I sat down in one of the chairs.

"Chris, we've got to talk."

"Not yet," I said.

I was trying to understand what I'd heard and what it meant. Verdoli was a multi-national electronics firm. They had a contract with the British Ministry of Defence. They didn't make it clear on the News, but it was something to do with a new generation of early-warning systems in the event of war. It wasn't just this country that was involved because the whole of NATO was interested.

But the Czechs suddenly started developing something similar for the Soviet bloc. It wasn't coincidence because a leak had been traced to the R and D Department in Verdoli's UK Division. Traced to Drew Smith. Father of my Smith. "My" in a manner of speaking, you understand.

They'd done a telephone interview with Derek Kellaway, Drew Smith's immediate boss, on TV. Kellaway sounded harassed. According to him, Smith was brilliant at his job. Kellaway kept saying that he couldn't believe it, that there must have been a mistake.

But there was more to it than that. Miss Tibberton used to work as a photographer for MI5. About two years ago she had a crisis of conscience and resigned. She talked about the dirty tricks in her job on a TV programme that was never shown, though everyone knew about its contents. And she'd allowed another ex-MI5 officer to quote her experiences in a book he wrote. The book was published all over the world except in this country. It caused a lot of fuss at the time.

They had to be careful what they said on TV but you could read between the lines. Miss Tibberton had escaped prosecution by a technicality. She'd set up as a freelance photographer. It seemed that Drew Smith had helped her get some work by recommending her to the PR department of a firm he used to work for.

It was easy enough to work out the implications. The authorities obviously thought that Miss Tibberton was involved in the spying, too. It wasn't likely that our people had killed her – why should they bother when they could destroy her credibility with an espionage charge? The people behind the killer had to be the Czechs, her new employers. She'd served her purpose and she knew too much about them.

And last but not least: the police urgently wanted to talk to Drew Smith's daughter, who witnessed the murder of Miss Tibberton but subsequently ran away. They flashed a picture of her on the screen: Smith in this dire school uniform, looking like something out of St Trinian's.

Alias woke up and jumped on to my lap. That broke the silence.

"They didn't mention you," Smith said. "That's something."

"No, it isn't – they know who I am from last night. And they know I was with you today."

"So why are they keeping quiet about it?"

I shrugged. "I reckon they're checking out the places I might be. You know, keeping it up their sleeve."

"Can they trace us here?"

I shrugged again. There was no way of knowing. Our house was empty. Judith thought I was with Barry. But if she and Clive were having a really good time together, the police might not be able to find her until tomorrow when she was meant to be coming home. Barry's parents, of course, had no idea that I was here. The big problem was Barry himself. I hoped to God he hadn't seen the News. If he had, there was a chance he wouldn't have recognized Smith: that school uniform made her look about three years younger than she was, and her hair was different in the photo.

"Barry's a friend of yours, isn't he?" Smith said. It was uncanny how she'd followed what was going through my mind. "He wouldn't rat on us."

"No way."

To be honest, I wasn't sure. I thought that, if the worst came to the worst and the cops got on to Barry, he'd hold out until he'd had time to talk to me. After all, we were mates. Well, only sort of, from my point of view. But as far as he was concerned, we were best buddies.

"So you think it's safe to stay here?" Smith went on. She seemed to have acquired this touching faith in my opinion. She also seemed to be taking it for granted that I was on her side. I didn't want to be on anyone's side.

"There's nowhere else to go," I said. "It's safer than spending the night on the streets."

"Dad's innocent."

"Oh sure," I said nastily.

Both of us spoke at a level that wasn't much more than a whisper. I was listening to the sounds outside: car engines, shouting and the occasional burst of disco music.

"He is so." The old aggressive Smith was back. But I didn't wilt because I wasn't the old me any more. I think she guessed that she wasn't getting anywhere – she went on in a gentler voice. "Let me tell you what happened, okay? What really happened."

"If you want."

"When I got home from school on Friday, Dad was worried. I've never seen him like it. When I asked him, he said it was a work problem. Yesterday morning he went into the office, which kind of surprised me. I get a week for half-term, and he was going to get the time off work. Next thing I knew, he called me and said I was to open the second drawer down in his bureau and find a blue envelope there. I had to take it to the person it was addressed to, and do what I was told."

"The person was Miss Tibberton?" I said. "Was that the first time you'd heard her name?"

Smith shook her head. "Dad talked about her once. Maybe a year ago. He was saying that she was being penalized for telling the truth. And that it couldn't have happened if this country had a Freedom of Information Act like we have in the States."

"Is it true he got her a job?"

"I don't know. It wouldn't surprise me. He's . . . the sort of guy who's a sucker for anyone with a hard-luck story."

I wondered if Czech agents had a good line in hard-luck stories.

"He told me that I had to leave the apartment by the fire escape and make sure that no one saw me. The only other thing was not to believe what people said about him. 'Trust me,' he said."

She screwed up her face and I thought she was going to cry again.

"What did Miss Tibberton say?" I asked quickly.

It turned out that Miss Tibberton had told Smith quite a lot, though not all at once and not in the right order. According to her, Drew Smith had realized that there was a leak at work, and he'd hired her to help him find out who was responsible. Some time ago, he'd done her a favour, and this was her way of repaying it. And she'd just come up with a piece of evidence that would nail the traitor. But the traitor was one step ahead: he – or she – had framed Smith's father and was now trying to silence Miss Tibberton and retrieve the single bit of evidence against him. He'd succeeded in every way but one: he hadn't got hold of the negative that was in Smith's pocket. Miss Tibberton, guessing that her flat might be searched, had hidden it at the zoo because it was near the studio flat she'd taken for a holiday. She hadn't been able to take the holiday because this business blew up. But she still had access to the flat.

100

It was just as well she did take the trouble to hide the canister.

"But it doesn't make sense," I said. "She could have taken the photo to the police. None of this need have happened. She needn't have died."

"I asked her that," Smith said quickly. Too quickly? "She told me that the police didn't trust her and she didn't trust them. Also that Dad wasn't just framed overnight – he'd have been set up as the fall-guy long ago. A kind of insurance policy if something went wrong. And I think there was another reason, but she wouldn't tell me what."

I glanced at her. Her face told me nothing I didn't already know. If what she'd said was true, her dad had played into the traitor's hands: going to Miss Tibberton would make him guilty by association in the eyes of the people who counted, which in this case would be Special Branch and MI5.

There was another point that really worried me. I'd have liked to find out if she'd realized that there might be a simpler explanation for Miss Tibberton's reluctance to go to the police. The official line might be true: she and Smith's father could be traitors.

"What was in the envelope?" I asked casually.

"Five hundred pounds in cash. Miss Tibberton gave me half, in case we got separated."

"Nothing else?"

She shook her head. Alias, who'd been assessing her for some time, threw an internal switch and stopped purring. It was like a power cut. In the silence, he jumped off me and on to her lap. She tickled him under the chin and he switched on the power again.

"When was her flat searched?" I said.

"She figured Friday night. She was out of town, you see, hiding the canister. She was expecting Dad to come round on Saturday afternoon. I turned up instead. Then you arrived."

"Why did you open the door?"

"To you?" She grinned. "Miss Tibberton thought you were the milkman."

"If you're right about all this," I said slowly, "then the bloke at the hospital today, the Spiderman, is either the traitor or . . ."

"The Czech spy he feeds the information to. Right."

There was something that didn't quite fit. "How did he get on to us so fast?" I went on. "I mean, we know that Gryson followed me but— "

"That's easy," Smith said impatiently. "He must have followed you too."

"Maybe." I wasn't convinced: if she was right there must have been a whole convoy on my tail that morning. I cleared my throat. There was something that had to be said, and I didn't want to say it. "You know this negative? You realize it could work either way?"

She didn't stop stroking Alias. For a couple of minutes, the only sound in the room was his purr.

"You mean it might not prove him innocent?" Smith said at last.

"I mean it could prove him guilty."

I felt as though I'd slapped her. I stared down at my hands rather than meet her eyes. But I knew I was right.

Anything could be on that negative. I didn't know much about microphotography and stuff like that, but I did know that Miss Tibberton had been an expert. Maybe the contents proved that she and Drew Smith were traitors. Only one thing was for sure: the negative was so important that the Czechs and Special Branch didn't care what they had to do to get their hands on it.

"I trust him," Smith said in a voice so low I could hardly hear. "I have to hang on to that."

"Yeah." I tried to smile. Our eyes met, and I felt a jolt go through me as though they'd collided somewhere in space midway across the room. I groped for the right words to say what I meant without saying too much. "We all have to trust people."

It sounded lame. Maybe I should have come right out with what I was feeling: that I trusted *her*. In the last few hours, things had changed. It wasn't just that I knew more about what was happening. It was also the fact that I'd started to like Smith. Two people can't survive a day like we'd had without getting to know each other.

As far as I was concerned, Smith was on the level. Maybe her father wasn't – but that wasn't my affair. I'd somehow started to rate her as a friend. I told myself that I didn't run out on my friends when they were in trouble. It sounded good. I almost believed it.

A small, cynical voice in the back of my head pointed out that, on the other hand, most of my friends weren't what Barry would call Enemies of the State. Nor was unarmed combat with plain-clothes policemen part of the price of their friendship.

I didn't listen to the voice. I'd finally chosen which side I was on, and I was staying there. I felt very tired.

"Tomorrow?" Smith said.

"We'd better leave early."

"And go . . ."

I nodded, noticing in passing that she was treating me as an equal. "It's the only thing left."

And if that failed, God knows what we'd do.

Smith lifted Alias off her lap and stood up. "We'd better get some sleep."

She looked half-dead on her feet. I stood up, too. The movement brought me nearer to her than I'd expected. In fact we were standing so close we were nearly touching. I was breathing faster than usual, though not for the same reason as before. I noticed all the details in her face as though I was examining it with a magnifying glass. The strand of hair that was caught on her cheek, the way the lips curved up at the corners, the shadows under the eyes. Blue eyes, with sort of greeny flecks in them.

"Good night," she said. "I . . . I'll get you a blanket."

After she'd gone to bed, I lay on the sofa with my feet over one arm and Alias on my stomach. I didn't want to sleep. I didn't want to listen to Paul Anders.

I just wondered if Smith was still awake.

CHAPTER FOURTEEN

It was the worst night I've ever had.

I was so tired that I should have been able to sleep like a log on the central reservation of the M25. But my brain wouldn't shut down. I was trying to plan our tactics for tomorrow. Like would it be better to phone first or just turn up? Like what happened if there was no one there? Like what would we do if the worst came to the worst?

There were no answers. I twisted and turned on that damned sofa, trying to get comfortable. Alias got fed up and went to sleep on a chair. I got up three times – once to go to the lavatory, once for some water and once because I thought I heard someone on the stairs. Each time I listened on the landing. Smith's door was closed. I couldn't even hear her breathing.

Night in London is never dark and never quiet. The city gives off an unhealthy yellow glow that infects the sky for miles around. The sound of traffic decreases but it doesn't die away. Any of those engines I heard could have belonged to a police car or a red Sierra.

The second time I got up I opened the curtains, so some of the yellow light seeped through the grimy window. When dawn came, I wanted to be the first to know. I hated the thought of tomorrow so much that I wanted to get it over as quickly as possible. The waiting was killing me.

My body had to have sleep if I was going to function properly in the morning. Knowing that made it harder to drop off. I tried the usual distractions, like planning the great pictures I was going to take one day and reciting all the Paul Anders lyrics I could remember. But for once most of the lyrics seemed like pretentious crap, and I couldn't even get enthusiastic about photography.

So I tried a new distraction: Smith. I was risking a lot for her, maybe even my life, so I figured it was sensible to find out why.

First, I decided, I liked the way she went on fighting. I couldn't think of anyone else I knew, male or female, who wouldn't have given in when Miss Tibberton crumpled to the pavement with a bullet in her. Also, I liked her because she made familiar things seem different. We spoke the same language, more or less, but when she said things they sounded special; maybe it was the American accent. When she wore my Paul Anders T-shirt, it was classy, like something with a three-figure price tag in a Mayfair shop. But when I wore it, it was just a T-shirt. And lastly, I liked looking at her. As a photographer, I mean. Smith had an interesting, *complicated* face.

Not like Dawn Fisher, who's about as complicated as a slap in the face. Dawn has one talent in life – attracting boys – and one interest – boys she fancies. If she likes you she giggles and if she doesn't she treats you like a serf. Compared to Smith she was downright boring.

At the time this conclusion felt like an earthshaking discovery. Right up there with the Theory of Relativity and the first men on the moon.

More to the point, Dawn Fisher succeeded where everything else had failed. The last thing I remember about that night was the thought that Dawn Fisher was overrated.

Someone was shaking me. Alias was howling as though someone had him on the rack. A grey morning light filled the room.

"That cat needs food," Smith said. "And I can't find the can-opener."

"Uh," I said.

"And the roof leaks in my room. Just above the bed."

It was raining again. The wind chucked a shower of rain against the window. Yesterday evening was still in the front of my mind. I didn't even have to remember it. I licked my lips.

"The tin-opener's in the carrier bag," I said. "At least it was last night."

She went away to find the tin-opener. Alias scampered in front of her, trying to trip her up. Stupid cat.

I rolled off the sofa and looked at my watch. It was nearly 7.30. My body ached. My head felt like it did after the one and only time I've been drunk. One Sunday afternoon, Steve and I raided his parents' drinks cabinet. Never again.

Ten minutes later I felt more normal. When I came out of the kitchen, my mouth glowing with toothpaste, Smith was watching Alias wolf his breakfast.

"I want some tea," I said.

Smith looked unsympathetic. "I want to see the newspapers. *Are* there newspapers on Bank Holidays?"

"A few, I think."

She was right – the more we knew about what was going on, the better. I volunteered to go and look for a newsagent. Secretly I hoped I might find a café that was open. Six takeaway teas and four fried-egg sandwiches would fit the bill. My mouth watered.

I put a carrier bag in my pocket and went out in the rain. I was soaked to the skin in about three minutes. I found a newsagent's but not a café. I bought all the papers that were on sale, and also some chocolate. The old woman behind the counter said I looked like a drowned rat and did I also want some water wings. Ha bloody ha.

I pretended to laugh. Lying on the counter was a picture of Smith on the front page of one of the papers – in ordinary clothes this time, and it looked just like her.

There was worse to come when I got back to the

flat and we ploughed through the papers. Smith found it first. She nudged my arm.

" 'Police say that the girl may be travelling with an English teenager named Chris Dalham. Dalham is known to be violent . . .' "

"Me?" I was so surprised my voice came out as a squeak. "Violent? Ah, come off it."

"Green Anorak," Smith said thoughtfully. "That's what did it. You got to think of this in terms of his ego."

One of the smaller headlines screamed at me: VERDOLI OFFER REWARD. They were offering £5000 for information leading to the discovery of Smith. I showed her the section.

"£5000? Is that all I'm worth? It's an insult."

The words were brave but her voice wasn't.

"We've got to get out of here," I said. "Now."

"What's the hurry?"

I was already on my feet, looking round for Alias. It shows what a state I was in: we should have ditched him.

"Barry," I said. "He'd sell his whole family for that sort of money."

For once I was standing no nonsense from Alias. He scratched and squirmed, but he was too dazed from breakfast to put up his usual resistance. I forced him into the basket and strapped down the lid.

Smith didn't waste time either. She went through the flat, chucking our stuff into the carrier bag that had held the newspapers. I opened the door at the head of the stairs.

"Chris," she said from the bedroom. "Come look at this."

She was standing at one side of the window, peering down at the street. The curtain must have concealed her from below. She backed away, letting me take her place.

At this hour the High Street was nearly empty. The rain had stopped. On the opposite pavement, a red-headed man was sweeping up broken glass. A green Rover was coming slowly down the road. At the far end, by the pub on the corner, a police car was parked.

The Rover drifted towards the kerb. We were too late. Barry had already talked and we'd run out of time again.

In a few seconds the trap would snap shut on us. We had one chance left.

Smith clattered down the stairs. I followed, carrying Alias. I had the sense to shut the door behind me. The lock was a Yale so there was no need to bother with the key. The door at the bottom of the stairs had another Yale.

In the yard we could hear a muffled thudding. They were hammering on the door at the end of the alleyway. It was made of heavy wood. I'd locked and bolted it on my way back with the papers.

The yard was covered with cracked asphalt and dotted with weeds and rotting vegetables from the shop next door. On either side and in front of us were brick walls, about fifteen feet high. That left the double gates at the back: eight feet high and topped with a strand of rusting barbed wire. They were made of two sheets of metal mounted on iron frames. The frames were strengthened with iron struts.

Smith rattled the padlock that held them together. I thought our luck had run out. Then she pulled my towel out of the carrier bag, held it in her teeth and climbed up the struts of the gate as though it were a ladder. She draped the towel over the barbed wire and stretched down a hand for the cat basket.

I passed Alias up to her. She lifted the basket over the top and let go. I heard it hit the ground and bounce. There was a screech of rage from Alias. I handed her the carrier bag and then started to climb the gate. Wood splintered behind me. Smith dropped down on the other side of the gate.

When I reached the top I had the sense to throw the towel down to Smith. If we left it there, they'd know which way we'd gone, and they wouldn't waste time breaking into the flat. It was a good idea but it had its disadvantages. As I hauled myself over, my jeans ripped and there was a stabbing pain in my leg. I let go.

It was a long drop and I landed awkwardly. The pavement shook the breath out of me. For a second I lay there, gasping. I heard running footsteps on the other side of the gates.

I scrambled up. Smith was already twenty yards away, running as fast as she could with the cat basket. We were in a straight, narrow road that ran parallel to the railway track, so there were no buildings on the opposite side. On my side there were more rear entrances to High Street shops and, right at the end, a block of flats. Some kids were standing outside the flats, and one of them was pointing at me.

I pounded after Smith. I realized later that we were luckier than we deserved. If Special Branch hadn't been in such a hurry, they'd have done a proper reconnaissance and covered the rear entrance. Later still, I realized that there was a very good reason why Gryson was in such a hurry.

"Where now?" Smith gasped as I overtook her.

I grabbed the basket. "Carry on. We'll reach the station."

I only had a rough idea of the layout of the area but I knew the way we'd come last night. At the end of this road would be the road we'd walked up last night, before we turned into the High Street. All we had to do was turn right and hope they hadn't got around to putting a watch on the station.

Our road swung round a 45-degree bend and there was the junction. It was a crossroads with traffic lights. Smith, who was in front, stopped so abruptly that I ran into her.

"Chris – get back!"

She seized my free arm and tugged me round the corner.

A red Sierra was standing at the crossroads, waiting for the light to change. I was close enough to read the numberplate. The three digits were the same as the end of our phone number. 941.

CHAPTER FIFTEEN

We must have walked for miles.

I thought I knew London pretty well, but we went through places I'd never seen before and I hope I never see again.

There was a pedestrian underpass beneath the railway. That led us into a huge housing estate where you couldn't see the concrete for graffiti. By this time we'd stopped running. Then we cut through a maze of old, terraced streets until we hit a canal that was used as the local rubbish tip. We walked along the towpath, past millions of depressed fishermen. The sun came out and I began to get uncomfortably hot. We took it in turns to carry Alias and the carrier bag. The towpath ran up to a road. And on the road, shimmering like a mirage in the middle of the Sahara, was a mobile sandwich bar.

It was too tempting. We joined the queue of disillusioned fishermen and eventually got served. We had breakfast – coffee for Smith, tea for me, and three sandwiches each – sitting on the rubbish-strewn bank above the towpath. Alias smelled the food and started miaowing.

"If we had any sense," I said viciously, "we'd drown that cat."

"We can't do that," Smith said. "He's a kind of mascot."

Stupid, sentimental girl, I thought, as I bent forward and pushed a crust through the grille of the basket. Anyway, I wouldn't have had the nerve to drop him in the canal, much as he deserved it. The cat was a pain but it wasn't him who was making me feel vicious, it was Barry.

Drowning would have been too good for him.

Smith grinned at me. She'd seen what I'd done with the crust. Then the smile vanished.

"But how did he know we were there?" she said suddenly.

"Who?"

"The Spiderman. It's like yesterday at the hospital."

She was right. It didn't make sense. All it did was make things even more complicated and—

"Sort of scary," Smith said.

The house we wanted was a semi-detached des res in a side road near the Heath. It was probably about the same size as my parents' house and worth at least ten times as much.

We got there around midday, after a long, roundabout journey on foot and by tube and bus. There were lots of cars and people around, most of them heading for the Heath and all of them in a holiday mood.

The house was painted white and the little front garden was crammed with flowers. Kellaway was a keen gardener. Apparently he was a bachelor and had time for a lot of hobbies.

"What sort of a car's he got?" I asked.

"I don't know. Something long and grey, I think."

There was nothing long and grey parked on either side of the street. Maybe he'd left it round the corner. Maybe he had a garage. We went up the path and rang the front-door bell.

There was no answer. We tried again. I kept glancing over my shoulder. "There's a yard out back, with a pergola," Smith said. "We had dinner there last summer. It's very private."

"Can we get to it?"

She wandered round the side of the house. A wooden fence blocked the way. There was a gate in it. Smith tried

113

the latch. It wasn't locked.

"And what do you think *you're* doing, may I ask?"

I nearly died of shock. Smith jumped. The words seemed to float down from the sky. I looked up. An old woman was sitting by the open window of the next house. When I say old, I mean about a hundred and fifty. She had a great curving nose that nearly met her chin and a mass of untidy grey hair. She also had a telephone handset in her left hand.

"Our Neighbourhood Watch Association is too efficient to be trifled with," she announced in the same booming voice as before. "Can you give me one good reason why I should not telephone the police?"

As I've mentioned before, I'm a good liar. Oddly enough, I'm best in a crisis. This time I didn't even have to think. I gave the old witch one of my frankest smiles.

"Well, I suppose my uncle might be a bit upset."

She put her free hand to her ear. "What was that? Don't mumble."

I repeated what I'd said at a much louder volume.

"Your uncle?"

"Mr Kellaway," I explained, maintaining eye-contact and giving her a souped-up version of the smile that works so well on our deputy headmistress. "We've come for lunch." The woman still looked suspicious. I wondered how well she knew her next-door neighbour. Maybe Kellaway didn't have any nephews. "Actually, he's a sort of cousin of my mother's, but we've always called him uncle."

"Really?" she said frigidly. But she was softening, I could tell.

"He's not back yet," I went on, "so we thought we'd wait in the garden. It's so nice with the – er – pergola."

The pergola registered. I just hoped that a pergola, whatever it was, could be described as nice. But I still

114

hadn't made the grade. Smith and I both looked pretty seedy. My jeans were torn and stained with blood and mud.

"And what's Mr Kellaway's Christian name?" she demanded.

"Derek," I said. Luckily they'd mentioned it in the papers and on TV.

The old woman lowered the telephone. "I suppose you can go and wait there," she said. I swear she sounded disappointed. "What have you got there?"

"That's our cat."

I angled the basket so she could see Alias through the top. The movement shook Alias awake, and he started savaging the wickerwork with his claws.

"Poor puss," the woman cooed. "Does Diddums want some foodie-woodies?" Her voice got tough again: "It's not fair to coop up a poor dumb animal like that."

"We're going away tomorrow," I explained. "Uncle Derek's going to look after it."

The interview was over. We slipped through the gate and into the garden. It was tiny but blazing with flowers. There was no grass but loads of old flagstones. At the bottom was a sort of green tunnel made of climbing plants trained round a wooden frame.

"That was brilliant," Smith whispered.

"I know. But what the hell's a pergola?"

She pointed at the tunnel. "The darkroom's behind it."

We looked at each other. Then we checked to see if the garden was overlooked from next door. It wasn't: the fences were high and an apple tree blocked the view from the hag's upstairs windows at the back.

The pergola was so densely covered that at first glance you wouldn't have guessed there was anything behind it. The entrance to the darkroom was round the side and heavily camouflaged by more vegetation. It was a small, brick building with a corrugated asbestos roof that was

115

covered with some sort of creeper. I guessed it had originally been used as a potting shed. Beside the door was a small window, covered with a black curtain. I tried the door. It was locked.

"Did you see the burglar alarm at the front of the house?" I said.

Smith nodded.

"You wouldn't expect it to include the shed."

"No," she said. "You wouldn't."

House-breaking doesn't come naturally to me so burglar alarm systems aren't one of my specialities. I had a vague idea that most of them consisted of an electronic circuit that linked the doors and windows of a house. If a burglar trod on a concealed pressure pad or passed through a light beam, the circuit would be broken and bells would start ringing. But who would bother to include a tatty old shed, half-concealed at the bottom of the garden?

"For all we know, Kellaway's gone out for the day. We could be here for hours."

"Trouble is," Smith said, "the old woman might hear the breaking glass."

"She's deaf. I had to shout at her."

There was another reason I was willing to take the risk: we had no guarantee that Kellaway wouldn't turn us over to the police as soon as he saw us. Smith was looking at me, and I could tell that the same thing was in her mind.

"Right," she said. "We'll use the towel. Maybe that'll muffle the sound."

Smith held the towel over the part of the window nearest the catch. We waited until there was a lot of traffic in the road at the front. Then I poked my elbow at the glass. Nothing happened, except that I jarred my funnybone. I tried again. The glass splintered with an almighty crack. Fragments tinkled on to the windowsill.

For thirty seconds we just stood there, waiting for an alarm bell or an armed posse of OAPs from the

Neighbourhood Watch Association. I grinned at Smith, put my hand carefully inside and opened the window. I pulled back the curtain and hauled myself over the sill.

The darkroom's layout was simple. One wall had the door and the window. An L-shaped counter ran round two of the other walls; in the corner was a small sink with hot and cold taps; above the counters was a row of shelves, and below them were cupboards. The enlarger, shrouded in a grey plastic cover, was on the end of the counter nearest the door. The fourth wall, which backed on to the pergola, was bare brick.

I unlatched the Yale and opened the door for Smith. There was so little space that there was hardly room for two of us inside. She dumped Alias on the counter; he'd gone back to sleep.

She handed me the film canister. "You don't need me. I'll keep watch by the gate." She touched my arm as she left.

The door closed behind her and I started thinking. I'd made contact prints, which are the same size as the negative, without much help before. But there was no point in doing a contact print now because we needed as much detail as possible. That meant using the enlarger.

The process is basically the same but I wasn't as familiar with it in practice. I twitched the cover off the enlarger. It's like a projector, mounted on a pole and pointing downwards. Kellaway's was older than Miss Tibberton's enlarger, but it seemed to work on the same principles.

The first thing I checked was the negative carrier. Luckily it was designed for 35mm, the same film size as our negative. I plugged in the enlarger at the wall socket and switched it on.

So far so good. I rummaged through the cupboards under the counter. There were 12" by 10" plastic dishes, which I'd need for the developer and the fixer. I found a measuring beaker for diluting the developer and a thermometer for taking its temperature. I couldn't find any

117

plastic tongs for handling the prints. My fingers would have to do. In the next cupboard was an alarm clock with a second hand and a safelight. I wound up the clock and tried the light.

The third cupboard contained a half-used packet of 10″ by 8″ bromide paper; it was the same as I usually use – Grade 2 with a semi-glossy finish. Beside it were some of Kellaway's prints. The one on top was an over-exposed and badly-focused shot of the Highgate skyline from Hampstead Heath. It cheered me up: even I could do better than that.

The chemicals were lined up on one of the shelves. The developer was Kodak D163. I had to mix the fixer myself.

The worst thing was the temptation to hurry. I had to force myself to go slowly. "Patience and method," Miss Tibberton used to say, "are the hallmarks of the professional photographer." As I worked, I muttered the words to myself over and over again. Even so, I cut every corner I could.

At last everything was as ready as I could make it. I switched on the safe light. With the curtains drawn, I opened the carrier and positioned the negative, emulsion side down, inside. I took the red filter from the enlarger's lens and turned off the overhead light. I didn't bother to check the negative for dust – I just slid the carrier into the head of the enlarger.

It was weird but I'd almost forgotten that Smith was outside, that Kellaway might turn up at any moment and that I was on the run.

Blurred shapes suddenly appeared on the baseboard. The easel was already set up for 10″ by 8″ prints. I adjusted the head so the image was the right size. Then I turned the knob that focused the lens. The image on the baseboard sharpened. It was upside down.

I swore and, glad that no one was watching, turned over the negative.

118

The photograph came alive. A crowd on the platform of a railway station. Maybe twenty people, standing in ones and twos, with the departures board towering above their heads. You had the sense that they were just a small section of a much larger crowd. A good photograph can tell a story, and this one was about trains being late in the rush hour. One man was reading a newspaper. He was built like a bull and you could only see his back. His face didn't matter – the point was, a real expert could probably enlarge the newspaper so much that you could work out the date from the page layout or even the headlines.

Then I saw the Spiderman. He was only a few yards away, half-facing the camera. I felt a stab of pure pleasure: we'd cracked it. He was talking earnestly to a small, podgy bloke in a light-coloured raincoat. The second man wore half-moon glasses and he had a high forehead: at present, that was all I could see of his face.

Suddenly I realized I had no idea what Drew Smith looked like; they hadn't shown a picture of him on the news. My satisfaction drained away. Almost mechanically I went on working.

First I raised the head of the enlarger to crop the image: I just wanted the Spiderman and his friend, and I wanted them as large as possible. I stopped the lens down to f8 and did a test strip to find the best exposure time. Fifteen seconds seemed about right. I positioned a piece of paper under the blades of the easel and exposed it.

It all went like a dream, maybe because I was acting like a sleepwalker. I pocketed the negative and slid the paper into the developer. As I rocked the tray, the stuff did its usual magic: the picture appeared, swaying beneath the surface of the liquid. I rinsed it carefully under the cold tap.

Just as I was about to dump it in the fixer, I heard steps outside. I swung round. The door was still locked and both my hands were full.

"Kellaway's here," Smith whispered. "He's with Gryson's woman. I'll hide outside."

As she spoke I heard the snap of the latch on the gate through the broken window. It was too late to open the door for her. It was too late to do anything but drop the print into the fixer, switch off the light and pray.

CHAPTER SIXTEEN

"You timed that well," Derek Kellaway said. "I've just got back from the office."

"Damage limitation?" For the first time I noticed that the fair-haired woman had a faint northern accent.

"That's the idea. It'll take months. He had a finger in most of our pies. Would you like a drink? I'm parched."

"Have you any Perrier?"

"Plenty. Shall we have it out here?"

The woman who looked like a horse must have nodded. I couldn't see them, of course, but they were no more than a couple of yards away and I could hear them so clearly that I might have been out there with them. One set of footsteps moved back to the house. I heard a creak and a sigh. There was a wooden bench in the pergola, and I guessed the woman had sat down.

I hoped that Smith was hiding in the tangle of vegetation by the door of the darkroom. If she was, she'd be out of sight from the pergola and most of the rest of the garden. But maybe she hadn't had time. Then there was the old dragon next door: she couldn't have seen Kellaway arrive, or we'd have known by now, but she might see him in the garden and mention his nephew. I gnawed my knuckles, which I always do when I'm tense. This time I tasted blood.

More footsteps and the chink of glass. Suddenly I realized how thirsty I was.

"You know, I still can't believe it," Kellaway went on. "It's like a bad dream. Drew was a friend as well as a colleague. Or so I thought. I take it there's no room for doubt?"

121

"There's always doubt. He hasn't admitted it, not yet, but the evidence against him is pretty strong."

"I never had the slightest suspicion . . ."

"Nor me. And I did his positive vetting. He was quite open about his politics. Made it quite clear that he only wanted to work on defence systems. The usual woolly liberal, I thought."

"A double bluff," Kellaway said sadly. "He's a clever man. I don't understand how the Tibberton woman fits in, though. Or shouldn't one ask?"

"That's one reason I came," the woman said. "I've been told to brief you about it. It's confidential, of course, but the Committee thinks you should know in case it affects your assessment of the possible damage. She used to be a pro, you see. One of us. She either knew or could have guessed what was important."

"So she was Drew's – what's the word? – control?"

"Not exactly. More likely the cut-out between him and the control. We've had to re-evaluate her. The current assumption is that she was a long-term Communist sympathizer. Probably run by the Czechs. But she never had access to more than low-grade information which they could get from other sources. Two years ago, we think, they decided she'd be more use to them as propaganda."

"Ah." Kellaway sounded amused. "So that's why she suddenly began to listen to the voice of conscience."

"She certainly caused a lot of damage when she went public – to prestige, as much as anything else. At the time we thought she was doing it off her own bat. And of course sections of the media presented her as a martyr, hounded by the authorities."

"And was she? Hounded, I mean."

There was a silence. The woman wasn't answering that question.

"But I quite see your point," Kellaway said smoothly, as if there hadn't been an awkward pause. "Drew *thought* she'd been hard done by, so he got in touch and offered to find her a commission?"

"Something like that. And of course the Czechs leapt at it once they realized where he worked. They must have suddenly realized that Tibberton still had her uses." She hesitated, and I heard the chink of glass again. "It might even have been the other way round: that the Czechs targeted Smith and used Tibberton to reach him, in which case the offer of work would just have been a cover story if someone noticed them together. But it doesn't really matter: the point is, Tibberton was the cut-out between the Czechs and Drew Smith. When we finally crack him, the odds are that he won't be able to tell us who his control was."

"But what was his motive?"

"Ideological? Financial? A bit of both? We haven't traced any payments but that means nothing. I don't know what makes a traitor." She laughed without amusement. "I leave that to the psychiatrists, who— "

Alias stirred in his basket. Just the faintest of creaks and the ghost of a miaow. The thumping of my heart became a couple of thousand decibels louder.

"What was that?" the woman said sharply.

"Just a bird in the tree, I think," Kellaway said. "There it goes. One of those damn pigeons. So who killed her?"

"The Czechs, of course. We think it went like this: Smith got wind of his arrest and sent his daughter to warn Tibberton. She told her control. They must have agreed to meet – how else would he have known where to find her? And he killed her before we could arrest her. Once we got hold of her, she'd have named him. He couldn't afford that. He's probably running about six other operations in this country alone. He's indispensable. She wasn't. But they must have been desperate – to risk a shot at a running target in a crowded street."

"A snapshot," Kellaway said absently. "That's what

123

hunters call it. Don't think me – ah – awkward, but how much of this is speculation? Have you any real evidence?"

"Enough. We've two unconfirmed sightings of a man named Vaclav Feranec. One near the scene of the murder and one near Tibberton's flat. Here – have a look at this. Ring any bells?"

There was another silence. I guessed she'd handed him a photo of Feranec.

"Not even faintly, I'm afraid," Kellaway said.

"He's tall – about six-three. Very long arms and legs."

The Spiderman.

"No, I'm sorry. Who is he?"

"He's attached to their trade mission. The usual cover. The fact he's doing the mopping up himself shows how vital a job it is. There's a rumour that he's under pressure from Prague. And now of course he's after the girl. Which is the other reason I wanted to see you."

"I don't follow. Why's he bothering with her?"

The bench creaked and Kellaway sounded nearer. Maybe he was standing up. A few slow footsteps: he was pacing up and down. If he took just a few steps round the corner he'd see the broken window or even Smith herself.

"Because Tibberton might have talked to her. Might have mentioned Feranec's name. And there's another possibility, though it's a bit of a long shot. The girl might have something that Feranec wants. Either from her father or from Tibberton."

That figured, I thought. It explained why Feranec had turned over Miss Tibberton's flat.

"Interesting girl. Came to dinner once, with Drew." Kellaway was speaking fast but he sounded as if he was thinking of something else. "I'll just get another drink. Would you like one?"

"Yes, please."

He was back in a couple of minutes. "There you go. You were asking about the girl. She had quite a lot to say for herself, the night she came here."

"No idea where she might go?"

"None at all."

"If Feranec gets to her first, she's as good as dead. But if we can find her, we'll be able to wrap up the whole operation. She probably knows far more than she thinks. *And* she'll be a lever to make her father talk."

"I must say I'm surprised that you haven't got hold of her already."

"So am I." The woman's voice was grim, like it had been on Saturday night when she gave Gryson a hard time. "We nearly got her this morning but she slipped through Gryson's fingers."

"So she's in London?"

"She was five hours ago. She's conned a boy into helping her – someone who knew Tibberton."

"I saw it in the paper this morning. But there's not much he can do for her, surely? Nuisance value, that's all."

The woman grunted angrily. "Rather more than nuisance value, I'm afraid. It's infuriating. They're just children, really. Gryson's co-ordinating the search. Any scrap of information comes straight to him. We've got unlimited manpower and we still can't find a couple of kids." She hesitated again, then added in a softer voice: "That's where you might come in."

"Anything I can do . . ."

"Put yourself in the girl's shoes. You're her father's friend. If she's seen the papers or TV, she'll know you haven't completely accepted his guilt. She's a stranger in this country. We've checked her schoolfriends and drawn a complete blank. She can't stay on the run for ever. She'll need money, shelter – advice, even. Sooner or later, she'll come to you. She's got no other choice."

"Good God. But couldn't she go to the US Embassy?"

"It's feasible. I wish she would. The Americans are working very closely with us on this, so we'd be the first to know. But if she was going to turn up at Grosvenor Square, she'd have done it already."

"So what do you want me to do?"

"If you hear from her, tell us. If she turns up, grab her and don't let go. And if you think of anything, anything at all, let me know."

"Naturally."

"I'll tell Gryson to put a team on the house, if you don't mind. Just in case."

"When will that start? I'd better stay here until you've got someone in position."

"I'll phone him from the car. He's at Victoria Square. Say thirty minutes, okay? To tell the truth, I'm surprised he didn't think of it before."

The bench creaked once more.

"I'm going home," the woman said. "Haven't slept for forty-eight hours. But call me if anything occurs to you. I'm the only Elizabeth Halstock in the book."

"I still can't believe it," Kellaway said again. "Not Drew."

"I find it hard to accept," Elizabeth Halstock said. "But that's probably because it means admitting I made a mistake in my assessment of him. Still, we can't argue with hard facts."

Two pairs of footsteps went down the garden. The latch of the gate clicked. I got ready to open the door. I was trying to think how the Halstock woman could be wrong. Out in the road, an engine fired: it sounded like the VW Scirocco GTi.

What Halstock had said was so watertight, so plausible, so *probable*. It all fitted. I'd been fooled all along – and so had Smith.

So who was the podgy man that Feranec was talking to in the photograph? If they were right about Miss Tibberton being the cut-out, it couldn't have been Smith's dad. A fourth person must be involved: it was the only answer.

126

All this went through my head in less than a second – my brain was revving like a car doing 30 m.p.h. in first gear. Only one thing was certain: I wasn't going to betray Smith. Not to Halstock, not to anyone.

I opened the door of the darkroom. She slithered inside and raised a finger to her lips. I guessed she'd reached the same conclusion as I had: that we had to keep our heads down until Kellaway was out of the way; we needed to talk.

"Yoo hoo! Mr Kellaway?" The booming voice was only slightly muted by the distance it had to travel from the front of the house. "Have you found your nephew? *Such* a nice lad."

There was nowhere left to hide and nowhere to run to. I switched on the light. No need to skulk in the dark – the shed was the first place he'd look. I didn't even bother to close the door.

"We've got to try and talk him round," I said urgently. The gate banged and Kellaway was coming down the garden, which was all to the good – he hadn't had time to phone the police. "And if not – well, there're two of us and one of him."

But Smith wasn't listening. She was peering at the print that was still lying in the fixer. And then Kellaway was standing in the doorway, and that was the worst shock of all.

You see, I'd seen him before. He was a small podgy man with a high forehead and half-moon glasses.

CHAPTER SEVENTEEN

"My dear," Kellaway said to Smith, "thank God you've come." He'd only run a few yards but he was panting so much that he could hardly speak. His eyes flickered round the darkroom, which suddenly seemed unbearably crowded. "I'm convinced your father's innocent, I've always said so. We must get you a lawyer . . ."

Smith just looked at him. In the last 48 hours I'd had some filthy looks from her, but this one was something else. If I'd been her, I'd have called him every name under the sun. But she didn't waste her breath: she shrivelled him with her eyes.

At that moment Alias woke up. He was hungry. He was tired of being cooped up in the basket. He flung himself at the bars and spat at Kellaway, who happened to be standing about six inches away.

Kellaway stepped away with unexpected speed, bumping into Smith. "What the devil—?"

The tray of fixer was inches away from him. He saw the photograph. The next thing we knew he'd skipped between us and was standing in the doorway. In one hand was the dripping photograph. In the other was something that looked like a short black stick.

"It's packed with lead," he said in a high, gasping voice, "and covered with rubber. If you know how to use it, you can break bones."

"You've blown it," Smith said. "The old woman knows we're here."

"I can handle that."

I'd finished up beside the cat basket. Alias flung himself at the grille. I pulled one of the straps through its buckle.

"What are you doing?" Kellaway snapped at me.

He was an instant too late. The grille fell open. Alias shot out of the basket in a foul-tempered blur of ginger fur. He wanted his freedom. He wanted to get back to the good life. He charged at the doorway.

Kellaway flinched. For just a second his attention was diverted. And in that second I dived for the hand that held the cosh. I wrapped both my hands round his wrist.

He was strong, despite his lack of height. He backed out of the darkroom, pulling me with him, and swung me against the jamb of the door. Then Smith plunged past me and grabbed his other wrist.

She rammed the hand against the wall. He grunted and staggered back. The photo fluttered to the ground. I let go of him and hit him in the stomach. Before he could recover, Smith and I were sprinting down the garden towards the gate. Alias had already vanished.

But we didn't have much of a lead – Kellaway was just behind us. Smith opened the gate. Suddenly all three of us pretended we were doing something else.

A uniformed police sergeant and a WPC were walking along the pavement. They glanced at us.

The sergeant murmured something to the WPC.

I turned, fighting for breath. "Goodbye, Uncle Derek." My voice was surprisingly calm. "Thanks for everything."

Kellaway glared at me. The old bat was at her window, observing the scene with interest. I gave her a wave, too. The two cops lost interest and walked on towards the Heath.

We started running up the road in the opposite direction. Kellaway didn't move.

"Is the young gel your nephew's girlfriend?" the neighbour asked.

I didn't hear Kellaway's answer. Smith snapped, "Hit the ground," and plunged on to the pavement in the shelter of a builder's skip. I followed. But not before i'd seen what she had seen.

129

A car had just turned into the road with a squeal of burning rubber. It was a green Rover.

"Well, I guess we're finished," Smith said. "I could scream and scream and scream."

"But we've cracked it. What's bugging you?"

We'd crossed Hampstead High Street and were walking south, through a tangle of side streets. Eventually, if we kept going, we'd reach Belsize Village and then Swiss Cottage. We still had problems but I reckoned we could solve them. I was feeling more cheerful than I'd felt for ages.

"For a start," she said, "Kellaway got the photo. No proof – who's going to believe us?"

I laughed. "He's only got the print. We've still got the negative."

Smith grabbed my arm. "Then we've still got a chance."

"More than that." I smiled at her but she didn't smile back. "We can just walk into any police station."

"No, we can't," Smith said slowly. "You heard what the woman said."

"But we've got *proof* that— "

"Haven't you worked it out yet?"

"Worked what out, for God's sake?" I didn't like her habit of treating me as if I had a mental age of six.

"It's very simple." She didn't seem arrogant any more – just tired, vulnerable and scared. "It's the only thing that makes sense. Listen."

By the time she'd finished speaking, I was no longer feeling cheerful. The sum total of everything we'd done was a big, fat zero. We'd reached the centre of the whirlpool and now we were going to drown.

"But we've got the negative," Smith went on.

"Yeah, but so what? It's useless."

"No. I said we've got a chance. There's still one thing we can do."

*

When at last we found a taxi, the driver refused to take us anywhere before he'd seen the colour of our money. I can't say I blamed him. We must have looked as if we'd been sleeping rough for days.

The address we'd tracked down in the phone book was in Bemish Road. I'd never heard of it but the driver said it was in Putney, south of the river.

I wanted to phone first but Smith thought it would be too risky. Both of us were as nervous as hell. During the drive we kept squirming round to look out of the back window of the taxi.

We drove over Putney Bridge, turned right by the lights and took the third or fourth road on the left. Most of the houses were little terraced cottages. There are lots of similar roads round our way – but with one big difference: the ones in Putney had been promoted into the des res category.

That made me think of Barry. Something twisted inside me.

"Number 19?" the driver said. "There you are." He glanced meaningfully at the meter.

While Smith paid him, adding a tip he didn't deserve, I got out of the taxi and scanned the road. A few couples were walking up from the river. There were plenty of parked cars but none of them was suspicious. I glanced at the house. Curtains were drawn across the two upstairs windows. A black cat was sitting on the sill of the downstairs window. I wondered where Alias was.

The taxi pulled away and Smith joined me by the gate. The cat looked disapprovingly at us as we walked up the short, gravelled path. I rang the bell and hammered on the door. There was a spyhole at eye-level.

Ten seconds later I tried the door again, and this time I didn't stop.

Smith opened the letter flap. "I can hear someone on the stairs."

"In a hurry, are we?" a voice said behind us.

We swung round. Detective Inspector Gryson opened the gate. His little mouth was smiling. He was alone.

The front door opened. Elizabeth Halstock frowned, first at us, then at Gryson. She was wearing a dressing-gown and her hair stuck up at all angles.

"Good afternoon, madam," Gryson said in his castor-oil voice. "Success at last."

"You'd better come in," she said.

Gryson moved towards us, shepherding us into the hall. We went into the long sitting room on the left. He stayed by the doorway, blocking the only exit. Halstock, who was standing by the fireplace, told us to sit down on the sofa.

"How did you do it?" she said to Gryson.

"We had a tip-off from Kellaway, just after you left him," he said. "They were hiding in a shed in his garden. They heard everything you said – including your name. They've come to turn themselves in. I'll take them back to Victoria Square, shall I?"

"No," Smith said. "He's lying."

"Enough of that." Gryson took a step towards us. "Time we were moving."

Elizabeth Halstock waved him back. She was looking at Smith. "What do you mean?"

"Gryson got to Kellaway's just after you left. Kellaway called him while you were there. It must have been when he fetched the second drinks. I was hiding just round the corner of the shed. I guess he saw my foot or something."

"Cut the crap, will you?" Gryson said. "You've wasted enough time already."

Smith ignored him. "We can prove it. The next-door neighbour must have seen us leave and Gryson arrive. All in a matter of seconds. Either Gryson's lying about

132

the tip-off or Kellaway called him long before you left."

"So what are you saying?" Halstock said.

"That Gryson's in with them. With Kellaway and Feranec."

"Do we have to listen to this nonsense?" Gryson bellowed. "Can't you see? She's just trying to get her dad off the hook. I was making a routine call on Kellaway and the tip-off was patched through to my car phone."

"Slandering Kellaway won't help your father," Halstock said coldly.

Suddenly I'd had enough. I had a vision of Gryson and Halstock putting Smith through a grinder and reassembling the pieces into a pattern that would suit themselves. Before I knew what I was doing, I was on my feet and shouting.

"Then maybe this'll help." I dug the canister out of my pocket and waved it in Halstock's face. "That's what they all wanted. It's a negative, right? Drew Smith hired Miss Tibberton to watch Kellaway. And she took a photo of him meeting Feranec. You know, the man he told you he'd never seen before. And how the hell do you think Feranec's been able to keep up with us? How did he know where Miss Tibberton was? Because Gryson was reporting back to him, that's why."

Gryson took another step forward. By now he was facing me in the middle of the room; Smith was sitting on his left and Elizabeth Halstock was on his right. "Of all the cock-eyed—" he began.

"That's a big allegation you're making," Halstock interrupted, looking at me. "If it's true, why on earth didn't you go to the nearest police station?"

"Because you told Kellaway that every bit of information about us went straight to Gryson. That negative would never have reached you."

"Let me have it," Gryson said impatiently. "I'll get it printed right away. It's probably one of the kid's holiday snaps."

133

"No, you don't." I backed away from him. "You'd just switch it for another 35mm negative."

Halstock held out her hand. "I think I'll have that."

"No," Gryson said. "Give it to me."

"Do as he says, Chris," Smith whispered jerkily. "*Please.*"

I looked at Gryson and understood. He had a small, black automatic in his right hand. It was pointing at Smith.

"Gryson," Elizabeth Halstock said softly. "You *fool.*"

"Throw it to me." He held out his left hand. "Gently."

I held on to it.

"It's too late," Halstock went on. She was amazingly calm. "You're finished."

"I don't think so." Gryson glanced at her, grinning. "No one knows I'm here. Except Kellaway, of course. When you don't check in at the office this evening, they'll send someone round. They'll find you and these two, that's all. No evidence, of course, but it's obvious what they'll think. Feranec or more likely his hit-man traced them here and shot you all, to hide the link between him and Drew Smith. They won't be able to prove anything. Proof's a luxury in this game, isn't it? And Kellaway and I will just . . . carry on as normal."

I'm a good liar. I'm at my best in a crisis.

"Not quite as normal," I said. "I made two prints from that negative." As I spoke, I noticed the rolls of fat that bulged over his collar. He didn't just bellow like a bull, he looked like one as well. A connection flashed like a spark in my mind. "You're in the photograph, too, aren't you? You're the man reading a newspaper. And I bet it was you who recognized Miss Tibberton when she took that picture."

It was an inspired guess but it hit him where it hurt.

"What have you done with the other print?" he said in a voice that made my skin crawl.

"If you kill us, you'll never know. Or not until it's too late."

I wasn't sure what I was trying to do. *Bull-baiting?* I was terribly afraid that I was just delaying the inevitable.

His control snapped without warning. The bull charged. He moved so fast there was nothing I could do. He seized my hand and twisted it. The canister fell to the floor. The butt of the gun collided with my cheekbone. Suddenly my legs were no longer supporting me. I hit the carpet with a thud. Gryson crouched down, took a handful of my hair and yanked my head up. With his other hand, he tapped the canister with the barrel of the gun so it rolled across the carpet towards him.

"Where's the other print?"

"Here," Smith said brightly. "Look."

Gryson glanced at her. It was the oldest trick in the book and he fell for it. In that instant, Halstock's left arm swept down in an arc. The chop caught him somewhere on the neck.

My head exploded with pain and, almost simultaneously, I heard the unexpectedly thin crack of the gun going off. I think I screamed. Gryson collapsed on top of me; he felt as hard and heavy as a double-decker bus. Harsh, stinging smoke mingled with the smell of his sweat.

"Chris," Smith yelled, "are you okay?"

I couldn't see anything, I couldn't speak and I couldn't move. Someone was fumbling on my left: I guessed that Halstock was getting the gun. It all seemed rather remote. I would have liked to have gone to sleep.

Halstock said something I didn't hear – I was too busy listening to Smith saying "Chris, Chris," over and over again, which was far more interesting. Then they hauled Gryson off me, handling him as if he was a dead weight. Suddenly everything was much more comfortable.

"Chris!" Smith was kneeling beside me, holding my head in her hands. "Say something, will you?"

She was paler than pale and her eyes looked bigger than I'd ever seen them. I had one of those odd thoughts you sometimes get when you're dreaming: it occurred to me that she was more real than anyone I'd ever met.

"Say something. Please."

"Uh." I cleared my throat and tried again. "I'm thirsty. I could murder a cup of tea."

Don't ask me why. She started crying.

CHAPTER EIGHTEEN

You'd think that the rest of what happened would be wonderful. It wasn't. In some ways it was almost worse than what had gone before.

Elizabeth Halstock said briskly that the bullet had just glanced off the bony part of my skull. A doctor would see me, of course, but in all likelihood, I'd just have a few headaches in the next day or two. Apart from that I had nothing more than the odd graze.

Meanwhile she ordered Smith to make some tea in the kitchen while she immobilized Gryson, who was still unconscious, with a couple of luggage ties. Then she got on the phone.

A whole convoy of vehicles turned up at Bemish Road. Smith and I were put in separate cars, and that was the last time I saw her.

I stood on the pavement, watching until her car disappeared round the corner. There wasn't much to see: just a white face framed by dark hair, staring at me through the rear window.

They took me to a bleak barracks of a place in Hounslow. There were more cups of tea, and endless interviews with people who rarely bothered to introduce themselves. Somewhere along the line they gave me a meal. Judith turned up and agreed, rather reluctantly, I thought, that I was her brother. I asked if I could see Smith, but they said it would be "Contrary to Standing Orders". Pompous gits. Then they told me to go to bed. The room they gave me was like a cell.

Elizabeth Halstock was right about the headaches. And the powder burns had ruined my haircut. What with that and the bruise on my cheek I looked like something left over from the Great Fire of London, which did nothing for my ego.

Next day there were more interviews. Halstock was there, and I have to admit she was slightly more human than the others. She told me that Smith and her father were now at the US Embassy, and all charges against him had been withdrawn. So Smith wasn't even in the same building as me.

In the afternoon my parents turned up. Apparently the RAF had flown them home from Gibraltar. They were in a real state, partly because I'd ruined their holiday but more because of what I'd got involved in. It would have been much easier if they'd started yelling at me. But they didn't.

They were allowed to see me in a grotty little room with four chairs and a metal table, all of which were screwed to the floor. My mother kept saying, "Thank God you're all right," while my dad, who looked grey beneath his sunburn, asked the plain-clothes policeman who sat with us questions he wouldn't answer. And I felt I was to blame for the whole mess.

The following morning they made me sign something and allowed me to go home. I couldn't talk to anyone about what had happened, especially not to journalists. My name had been in the papers on Monday morning: if anyone asked about it, I was to say it was another Chris Dalham, not me.

Elizabeth Halstock drove me back home. On the way she tried to explain why all this was necessary in the interests of national security. She didn't convince me, but at least she tried. I asked her if the Smiths were going to stay in the UK or go back to the States. She said she didn't know.

A little while later I said, "Why didn't Feranec kill Smith in the hospital car park?"

She hesitated so long that I began to think she wasn't going to answer. "He needed that photo. When he shot Miss Tibberton, he knew that Gryson would be the first to search the body. He had to shoot her. If she'd been arrested, she'd have talked – Gryson couldn't have stopped her. When they realized she didn't have the negative, they went after Smith."

"Because she was the only person who might know where the negative was?"

Halstock grunted.

"So if Gryson had been around in that car park, Feranec might have shot her?"

Another grunt.

"Why didn't Drew Smith tell you he suspected Kellaway?"

"Ah – as a matter of fact he did."

I glanced at her. She looked a little pinker than usual.

"But you didn't believe him," I said.

"All the evidence pointed the other way. He didn't even know about the photograph. It was only taken on Friday evening, you see."

We turned on to the North Circular. I tried to keep the conversation going.

"What will happen to them?"

"Gryson will stand trial. You may have to give evidence, I'm afraid."

"And the others?"

"Kellaway skipped the country. Sooner or later, he'll probably turn up in Prague or East Berlin or Moscow. Feranec we can't touch – he's got diplomatic immunity, and anyway he's back in Prague." She sniffed. "A lot of damage, a lot of work, and not much at the end of it."

"At least the wrong man isn't going to be convicted."

She glanced at me as she slowed for a traffic light. "You're right." For the first time she smiled. "In my line of work, we tend to forget little things like that."

We drove the rest of the way in silence.

Being at home was like one long funeral. I was almost glad to get back to school. That was stupid of me.

Barry blamed me for fooling him, which was fair enough, and for his failure to get the £5000 reward, which wasn't. I'd left my Walkman and a Paul Anders tape at his dad's flat. When I asked him for them back, he said they weren't there. He'd probably sold them already.

Even worse, he'd spread a rumour that I was acting as a police snout. In my school that sort of rumour makes you an outcast. I couldn't even tell them the truth, that the only police informer on the loose was Barry himself. I knew in the end I could sort it out, but that wasn't much comfort in the short term. Who needs enemies when you've got friends like Barry Sinclair?

All the time I had Smith in my mind, like an anxiety that won't go away. For two days we'd been closer than I'd ever been to anyone. When they drove her out of my life, she left a vacuum behind. I even looked up Smith in the phone book, which was a waste of time as there were about a million Smiths to choose from. In any case, perhaps she wouldn't want to see me. Maybe I was tied up with too many unpleasant memories.

When I got home from school that first day, my mother said a letter had come for me by second post. I glanced at the envelope on the kitchen table and suddenly it was hard to breathe. The handwriting looked like a row of four-legged spiders.

"Oh yeah?" I said. Really casual. I don't think I fooled my mother or Judith.

I didn't want to open the letter in front of them or even in the same house. I put it in my pocket and said I was going for a walk.

To be honest, I was scared to open it. Sounds stupid, doesn't it? I felt as though I was standing on a precipice, and whatever Smith had written could either push me over

140

the edge or draw me back to safety.

It was a dull, grey evening. Every now and then there was a low mumble of thunder. I didn't notice where I was going. I didn't notice anything until I turned into Endymion Street and heard a loud miaow.

Alias was sitting on the low wall outside number three. He looked plumper than ever, and he was wearing a smart green flea collar.

For once I gave him all the attention he needed. He purred and writhed for about five minutes while the thunder came closer and closer.

"Peter!" It was a woman's voice, somewhere at the back of the house. "Sup-sups!"

Alias cocked his ears. A fork rattled against a tin. He stopped purring. I'd suddenly become invisible to him. He jumped down from the wall and ran down the alley at the side of the house.

Alias had become Peter. Against all the odds, he'd rediscovered the good life.

It started to rain – great big drops that drenched everything in sight in seconds, including me. I was back where it all started – getting wet on the corner of Endymion Street. But nothing was really the same as it had been on the Saturday afternoon when I found Pseud's body and met Smith for the first time.

All that was over. So I turned round and went back to the main road. I sheltered in the doorway of a shuttered shop.

Then I stopped feeling sorry for myself and opened the letter.

The Pit

ANN CHEETHAM

The summer has hardly begun when Oliver Wright is plunged into a terrifying darkness. Gripped by fear when workman Ted Hoskins is reduced to a quivering child at a demolition site, Oliver believes something of immense power has been disturbed. But what?

Caught between two worlds – the confused present and the tragic past – Oliver is forced to let events take over.

£2.50 □

Nightmare Park

LINDA HOY

A highly original and atmospheric thriller set around a huge modern theme park, a theme park where teenagers suddenly start to disappear . . .

£2.50 □

ARMADA

Run With the Hare

LINDA NEWBERY

A sensitive and authentic novel exploring the workings of an animal rights group, through the eyes of Elaine, a sixth-form pupil. Elaine becomes involved with the group through her more forceful friend Kate, and soon becomes involved with Mark, an Adult Education student and one of the more sophisticated members of the group. Elaine finds herself painting slogans and sabotaging a fox hunt. Then she and her friends uncover a dog fighting ring – and things turn very nasty.

£2.50 ☐

Hairline Cracks

JOHN ROBERT TAYLOR

A gritty, tense and fast-paced story of kidnapping, fraud and cover ups. Sam Lydney's mother knows too much. She's realized that a public inquiry into the safety of a nuclear power station has been rigged. Now she's disappeared and Sam's sure she has been kidnapped, he can trust no one except his resourceful friend Mo, and together they are determined to uncover the crooks' operation and, more importantly, find Sam's mother.

£2.50 ☐

ARMADA

Armada
Gift Classics

An attractive collection of beautifully illustrated stories, including
some of the finest and most enjoyable children's stories ever
written.

Some of the older, longer titles have been skilfully edited and abridged

Little Women	Louisa M. Alcott	£2.25
Peter Pan	J. M. Barrie	£2.25
The Wizard of Oz	L. Frank Baum	£1.95
Lorna Doone	R. D. Blackmore	£1.95
What Katy Did	Susan M. Coolidge	£2.25
What Katy Did at School	Susan M. Coolidge	£1.95
What Katy Did Next	Susan M. Coolidge	£1.95
The Wind in the Willows	Kenneth Grahame	£2.25
The Secret Garden	Frances Hodgson Burnett	£2.25
The Phantom of the Opera	Gaston Leroux	£1.95
The Railway Children	E. Nesbit	£1.95
The Scarlet Pimpernel	Baroness Orczy	£1.95
Black Beauty	Anna Sewell	£1.95
Kidnapped	R. L. Stevenson	£1.95
Treasure Island	R. L. Stevenson	£1.95
Dracula	Bram Stoker	£1.95
Gulliver's Travels	Jonathan Swift	£1.95
The Adventures of Tom Sawyer	Mark Twain	£1.95
Around the World in 80 Days	Jules Verne	£2.25

ARMADA